PRAISE FOR WHEN I'M WITH YOU

This was such a sweet read, I finished it in one sitting. Elizabeth and Ryder's childhood history makes their chemistry feel instant and natural. They respect and support each other so well, even when it means stepping back. And now I'm even more excited to see what's next in Hearts Bend. I just love this little community.

— JO|RUTH READS, GOODREADS

I loved *When I'm With You* by Rachel Hauck. Fraud, fires, family, chemistry, and second chances in a delightful small town kept me reading way past my bedtime! A wonderful romance in a small town I'd love to live in!

— JEANNE, GOODREADS

What a charming small town romance. Elizabeth and Ryder's story is a delightful read about friends to more. Fans of small town romance, especially Hearts Bend, will love *When I'm With You.*

— ALLYSON, GOODREADS

HEARTS BEND ROMANCES

Home to Hearts Bend

When I'm With You

Anyone But You

What If I Stay

Hearts Bend

The Wedding Chapel

The Wedding Shop

The Wedding Dress Christmas

To Save a King

WHEN I'M WITH YOU

HEARTS BEND || BOOK ONE

RACHEL HAUCK

When I'm With You
Home to Hearts Bend, Book 1
Published by Sunrise Media Group LLC
Copyright © 2026 Rachel Hauck
Print ISBN: 978-1-966463-67-2
Ebook ISBN: 978-1-966463-68-9

This book is a work of fiction. Names, characters, places, and incidents are either products of the author's imagination or used fictitiously. Any similarity to actual people, organizations, and/or events is purely coincidental.

Scriptures taken from the Holy Bible, New International Version®, NIV®. Copyright © 1973, 1978, 1984, 2011 by Biblica, Inc.™ Used by permission of Zondervan. All rights reserved worldwide. www.zondervan.com The "NIV" and "New International Version" are trademarks registered in the United States Patent and Trademark Office by Biblica, Inc.™

For more information about Rachel Hauck please access the author's website at the following address: www.rachelhauck.com.

Published in the United States of America.
Cover Design: Sunrise Media Group LLC

For Dad who always said,
"Rachel, you're a writer. Be a writer."

HOME TO HEARTS BEND

Hearts Bend is an exciting, small southern town hosting the likes of an NFL quarterback and country music superstar. Hearts Bend is also "hometown" to Prince John, Princess Gemma and Princess Imani from Rachel Hauck's True Blue Royal Series. To learn more, visit www.rachelhauck.com.

HEARTS BEND
Ashland City
STAR FALL ROW
Two Daisy Acres
Christmas Shoppe
Rockmill High
Oshay Shirts
Hearts Bend Bank
Wedding Chapel
Pops Yer Uncle
MERCY RD.
RIVER ROAD
Cumberland River
WILLOW WAY
Angelo's Pizza
WILLOW PINE
Roseanne's Vintage Shop
Haven's Bakery
Scott's Farm
Gardenia Park
Cooper's Grocery
Valentino's
FIRST AVE.
Kids Theater
GARDENIA CIRCLE
OX HOLLOW
INN ROAD
Fry Hut
FRY HUT
Ella's Diner
BLOSSOM ST.
Wedding Shop
OLD MAIN ST.
Hearts Bend Inn
City Hall
Java Jane's
40 Nashville

1

Hearts Bend, TN

All her life, she'd believed that if she worked hard enough, she'd achieve her dream. That's what *they* said. And in so many ways, *they* were right. Except *they* forgot to mention life's curveballs. Situations beyond one's control.

Yet Elizabeth Dorsey refused to go down without swinging. This spring, she'd finally knocked one of her curveballs out of the park and graduated from MIT with honors. Then another strange pitch—maybe a knuckleball this time—sent her back to the dugout. Her dream of attending the Wharton School for her MBA was waitlisted.

Not to worry. She'd learned a lot in the past five years.

Parking her car along the curb of Lilac Street off River Road and under the shading maple near her grandparents' home—a mid-century modern meets two-story rambler—in Hearts Bend, Tennessee, she grabbed her backpack and headed up the walk.

She'd been here a month, but some days it felt like forever. Even worse, this *might be* her forever. When she walked across MIT's stage wearing honors regalia for her Bachelor of Science in Management degree, she believed one thousand percent that her next move was an MBA from the Wharton School. Not working in the financial office of the family-owned Dorsey Furniture.

"Beth?" Granny peered out the kitchen door as Elizabeth hung her backpack in the mudroom. "Dinner's on the table."

"No time. Tina called. Asked if I could come in at six." She set her lunch containers in the sink. Granny's cooking made for fab leftovers. "I'll wash those later."

"You know I love Tina, but I hope you told her six nights in a row was too much." Tina Danner was a dear friend and owner of the town's beloved Ella's Diner.

"Of course not. I like working." Her experience would aid her coursework once she made it into Wharton. Elizabeth grabbed a chicken leg from the table as she headed for the stairs. "The night manager no-showed, and Tina has to be at a grandkid's birthday bash."

If she wasn't working, what was Elizabeth going to do—sit at home and watch TV with Granny and Pops? She couldn't put that on her résumé.

Working at Ella's Diner felt like home away from home. She'd waitressed at the Hearts Bend diner during her high school summers. Tina had once told Granny no one had ever worked as hard as Elizabeth. So naturally, even at twenty-five, she had a reputation to uphold.

"Fine," Granny called up after her. "But do you have time to sit down and eat? One chicken leg won't do."

"Good news, Granny, Ella's serves food." Elizabeth changed from the slacks and blouse she'd worn to Dorsey Furniture into her diner uniform—an Ella's T-shirt, jeans, apron, and a pair of Hokas.

"Yes, but is it your granny's food?"

"Nothing is my granny's food." She tucked in her T-shirt and tied her sneakers.

Down the hall, she washed her face, braided her hair, and gave herself a pep talk via the mirror. "Forget your messy room. Focus on your task. Outperform your expectations. Show the world you're ready for the next level."

Granny met her by the back door with a baggie of carrots. "Here. Munch on these. I have to know you're getting something healthy."

"I had leftover salad and grilled salmon for lunch, and four cups of coffee. Isn't that healthy?" She had Granny with the coffee remark. She and Pops were coffee freaks. Three or four mornings a week, they drove to town for a walk in Gardenia Park before heading over to Java Jane's for a cup—or two or three—of joe.

"Three is fine, but four is over the line." She shimmied the baggie. "Eat these on your way, and have Tina's great chicken soup on your break. And come home early if you can. I hate how much you're working. Are you sure you're not wearing yourself out? You know the doctor—"

"I know what the doctor said. I'm being careful." Elizabeth snatched the baggie and headed for the kitchen door. "Granny, everything seems easy after MIT."

Through the mudroom, she picked up her backpack

and headed out. After the high of MIT, earning her degree with expectations of Wharton, the hardest part of moving to Hearts Bend wasn't the long hours. It was feeling like a failure.

When her application to Wharton was wait-listed—wait-listed!—she'd accepted a job at a Boston marketing company, only to learn two days before her start date that they were cutting staff. Drastically.

That's when Dad casually tossed out the idea of working in the family business to gain experience. He'd worked there for a year after graduating from Ohio State. Then he got the job in Boston and never looked back.

While she hated any further delay to her plans—most of her friends were already in grad school, launching amazing careers, even getting married or having kids—the whisper in her soul told her she needed this break. And the experience would be good.

Ducking into her classic '73 Volkswagen Super Beetle—a graduation present from her parents—with its candy-apple red paint glistening in June's early evening light, Elizabeth fired up the engine, stared out the windshield, and uttered her mantra.

"Don't let another setback define you. Just keep going."

Heading down River Road with the restored car's new A/C system blasting, Elizabeth let Blake Shelton sing away her cares. *Try to remember the good things, Beth.*

Living with Granny and Pops was always fun. Getting reacquainted with her boisterous, nosy, loving extended family was half annoying and half a blast. Working in the finance office of Dorsey plus nights and weekends as a manager at Ella's was more energizing than she thought.

But any day, *any day* now, she'd hear from the Wharton School's admissions office.

No flies on that girl. We made a mistake wait-listing her.

At the stop sign, Elizabeth shifted into first with a sigh. The heat waves rising off the road felt like her own weariness. Blake's song ended as she let off the clutch and turned right onto First Avenue. Miranda Lambert came on, encouraging her to kick butt and take names.

"I'm trying, Miranda."

She could deal with being tired. She'd excelled at pushing through tired. First, when she was sick for so long, interrupting her college career, then with her MIT course load. Colleges should hand out "Survived Tired" medals along with the diplomas.

A bang resonated from under the car, and the Beetle Bug swerved hard to the right. Elizabeth gripped the steering wheel and, with one foot on the brake and the other on the clutch, eased to the road's shoulder.

A flat. Of all things. Walking around to the front, she knelt to inspect the damage, then popped the trunk. No spare. Dad told her to get one, but she forgot. She closed the lid, her exhaustion creeping higher.

Now what? She could call Pops or one of her cousins. But calling a Dorsey meant the whole family would get involved in this very minor incident. Dad and Mom would hear up in Boston, and Aunt Raelynn down in Jacksonville. Dad would text, "You didn't get a spare?"

Peering down the road, she retrieved her backpack, locked the doors, and started jogging toward town. She'd been meaning to take up running.

On the way, she called Tina. "Hey, had a bit of car trouble—No, I'm fine. Flat tire." She refused to admit she was hoofing it. Tina would send the fire department. "I'll be there in a few."

Hanging up, she picked up her pace. Calling for help had been a way of life for two long years. So for now, if it was okay with the rest of the world, she'd like to take care of herself.

❦

It was good to be back home. Ryder Donovan raised his binoculars to scan a local camping area from the top of a dilapidated Cheatham Wildlife Management Area fire tower.

The weathered boards were twenty-seven years old and starting to rot. He had to skip every other step to rise to the top, but this was one of his favorite places in the whole reserve.

Yeah, sure, aerial surveillance did most of the fire-watching these days, but Ryder still preferred to climb the tower. Something about its ancient purpose connected him to all the rangers and officers who'd gone before him, watching over and protecting American soil.

From his perch, he had a good view of Cheatham Lock and Dam, the surrounding summer trees, and the picnic area where folks liked to spend a lazy afternoon stretched out in the shade.

Moving to his right, Ryder spotted a family packing up their campsite in the Right Bank Recreation Area. He zoomed in on the black coals of a firepit just as one of the male campers came around with a bucket of water. Good. Good. They'd seen the fire warnings posted throughout the reserve. It'd been what, five weeks since Middle Tennessee had a decent rain? Another week or two and they'd issue a fire ban.

The landscape of Middle Tennessee was nothing like the majestic Rocky Mountains, but the scent in the breeze, the miles and miles of lush green within Cheatham grounded Ryder to who he'd been. And maybe who he wanted to be.

He was climbing down the tower when his radio squawked. "Ryder?" It was Rick Haridopolos, his buddy, working the lake today, checking fishing licenses. "Go to five."

Ryder switched the channel. "What's up?"

"Just came from the office. Travis, man, you know he's been on the warpath. Today he came in ranting and raving about the loggers hired to clean up after the storm. They cut down about fifty grand worth of white oak. Some of the oldest on the grounds."

"What?" One tree was guessed to be at least a hundred and twenty-five years old. "How'd that happen?"

"Travis swears up and down you hired the guys. Without a contract."

Ryder laughed, waiting for Rick to admit he was kidding. "Wait, you're serious? I don't contract workers."

"Also, Travis claims you purchased some cherrywood from Dorsey? And some chicken baskets from Ella's Diner for the kids' fire-safety hour."

"The chicken baskets, yes, but cherrywood? What would I do with cherry?"

"Fix up your house? Use it on the fire tower?"

Ever since he moved back to Hearts Bend from Colorado, his boss, Travis Vermeer—who hired him, by the way—scrutinized everything he did. Almost as if he suspected Ryder of sabotage. Initially, Travis had been angry when Ryder submitted a request to the Tennessee Wildlife Resources Agency to repair the fire tower. He claimed Ryder had gone over his head. Made him look bad. Apparently, the tower should've been repaired years ago.

"Thanks, Rick. I'm coming in."

Ryder returned to the station, nodding to Travis's secretary when he entered. "Is he around?" Might as well get it over with.

"Yep." Cheryl tipped her head toward the office door and winked at him, her eyes heavy with false eyelashes. "And he's in a mood."

"So I've heard." Ryder knocked on the director's door. "You wanted to see me?"

Travis looked up, the skin under his chin jiggling, and tossed a piece of paper to the other side of his desk. "What's the meaning of this?"

———— ♥ ————

She wasn't going to make it. She'd die right here on First Avenue, mere blocks from Ella's Diner.

Water…water…

Why didn't she call for help? If Granny knew she got out of her car and ran down the side of River Road to First Avenue and the center of town, she'd give her a piece of her mind. And then some.

You'll wear yourself out! she'd say, worried. Yet it'd been two years since—

A siren blip startled Elizabeth off the sidewalk. When she turned around, a Hearts Bend police car eased along the curb.

"Hey, Beth." The officer leaned over the passenger seat to peer up at her. "That your car on River Road?"

"Yes, and what's the big idea of scaring me half to death?" The police officer, her cousin Jeff Simmons, had been one of her best friends as a kid during her summers-in-the-South days.

Jeff pushed open the door. "Get in. I'll drop you at Ella's."

"And have people think you arrested me? I don't need that rumor landing in the Wharton admin office."

"No one will think I've arrested you. And it was *people* who called me to say your car was on the side of the road."

"Who's calling you?"

"People who know you're the Dorsey who drives a classic red VW Bug."

"Fine." Elizabeth tossed in her backpack and dropped into the passenger seat. "I'm not sure I like *people* knowing my business."

In the world of social media, all it took was a person tagging her on some post about riding in a cop car and Wharton would find out. However, she *was* tired. And late. Tina's grandkids meant the world to her, and Elizabeth didn't want her to miss the party.

Jeff headed east toward the center of downtown Hearts Bend, past Angelo's Pizza, Cooper's Grocery,

Gardenia Park, and the historic Wedding Shop. "What's your plan for the flat?"

"Fix it. But Jeff, you're not obligated."

Growing up in Boston, Elizabeth was the Dorsey cousin from the city. Hearts Bend Dorseys were the country cousins. And country cousins pitched in to help, fix, and counsel.

"Okay," Jeff said in his lighthearted way. "But I do feel obligated to impound it."

"Jeff Simmons, you'd better not."

"It's Officer Simmons to you."

"Whatever." Elizabeth glanced over at him, laughing. "I was going to look up a service truck when I got to work. And if you haul off my car, I'll tell Granny."

"Ooo, ladies and gents, she pulls out the big guns. But knowing Granny"—Jeff reached for his radio and, with a couple of clicks and code words, ordered her a tow truck—"she'd be on my side. Also, your car will be at Marty's Garage. You can pick it up after work."

"At eleven o'clock? He'll be closed. How will I pay?"

Jeff waved off her question. "Ah, no worry. Marty will find you. Or one of us."

"You're not paying for my new tire. What is with this family and—"

"A little overwhelming, is it?" Jeff turned onto Gardenia Circle, slowly cruising around the park while responding to a radio call. "Having so much family around when you're used to living in Boston, away from us most of your life."

"Everywhere I turn, there's a Dorsey family member, or worse, a Dorsey friend. Some lady walked up to me at Cooper's last week, asked how I was doing. Was I feeling better? Said her nephew had Epstein–Barr, and it really knocked him for a loop. Never saw the lady before in my life. Never mind all the people who remember me from when I was a teenager, working at Ella's. It's like living on a reality show."

"Welcome to Southern hospitality."

"You've become more hospitable since I was last here," Elizabeth said, though she really didn't mind Hearts Bend's Southern ways.

"We've missed you, Beth. And for a long time, we didn't even know what was going on with you. And the lady in the grocery store was probably in Granny and Pops's prayer group."

"I didn't want anyone to know." There's no shame in being sick. She just didn't want any labels. To be the girl with the virus that never really went away.

"So we heard." Jeff pulled into one of the angled parking spots in front of Ella's. "You like your privacy, don't you?"

"Yeah, a little." She'd always been protective about her thoughts and feelings, even more so after being sick. But lately, being private felt more like a burden.

"I'm the opposite. During college, I struggled with that alone-in-a-crowd feeling and hated those first few months on campus, not knowing anyone. I kept it to myself, but eventually told Granny."

Elizabeth tried to imagine her handsome, gregarious, teddy bear of a cousin wandering a college campus alone. "My guess is you weren't lonely for long."

"I made friends, found a place to fit, but none of it ever felt like home, like being with the family in a town where everyone knew me. Or so it seemed."

"Is that why, after four years of education, you chose to be a police officer?"

"I tried corporate life. Moved to Dallas for two years. Then took a stint at Dorsey Furniture. It wasn't for me. Being a cop makes me feel like I'm giving back. Besides, I have politics in mind for the future. I'll use that ole Vanderbilt degree one day. So, you're still Wharton-bound?"

"Naturally." She'd not told anyone she was in Hearts Bend because she was wait-listed. Only that she wanted more real-world experience before starting school. The pre-term exercises would be about her work experience.

"How do you like working for Dorsey Furniture?"

"I like it. Will's a good boss. The atmosphere is fun yet professional." Will was another Dorsey cousin and now the CEO of the family business. "Seeing things from the inside puts reality to all the stories we heard as kids. Sometimes I think Dad wishes he'd stayed here, worked with his siblings. But his opportunities came in Boston." Elizabeth reached for her backpack. Now she was really running late. "I like to think I inherited the Dorsey ingenuity and vision."

"I'm sure you did, Miss MIT-with-Honors grad. Granny was popping her buttons when she told us you were coming down for the summer. Called it a miracle."

"Thanks for the ride, Officer Simmons." Elizabeth popped open the car door.

"Hey, give me your keys. We'll have someone bring your car around when it's ready."

"My keys? I see your master plan. To steal my car. I saw you eyeing it the other day at Granny's." Nevertheless, she dug the keys from her backpack and tossed them over. "No donuts in empty parking lots."

"Really? Not even one?"

Elizabeth hurried into the diner. Jeff was her favorite cousin. But so was Will. And Ethan. Truly, she loved them all. They made her laugh. Treated her like year-round family.

Nevertheless, she had to get used to all the family togetherness. She grew up with just her parents and brother, Jonathan. Dad and Mom raised them to be independent. She never asked for help with menial tasks. Until she contracted Epstein–Barr. Now that she was better, she wanted to be strong. A woman who stood on her own.

"Tina, I'm here. You can go." Elizabeth made her way through the kitchen toward the bank of lockers. She tossed in her backpack and grabbed her Ella's ball cap. "I'd still be running if Jeff hadn't picked me up."

"I was about to send Cade after you." Tina pointed to the young, skinny high school kid mopping the back of the kitchen. "Then you came in." She handed Elizabeth the controls to the server's pagers and the window checklist. "I called Marty. Told him to give you four of their best new tires, keep an old one for a spare, and send the bill to me."

"What? Tina, you're not paying for my tires. It's my car."

Tina loaded a plate with hot fries and shoved it under a heat lamp, then paged the server. "Friends take care of friends in this town. Besides, you've worked a lot of extra shifts for me, and you've only been here a month." She squeezed Elizabeth's shoulder. "And you'll need money for grad school. I *am* doing this." She turned toward the service window. "Hey, Lucy, did you see your plate is up? Are you wearing your pager? I didn't give it to you for decoration." Tina freed her long, silver hair from under her cap and motioned for Elizabeth to follow. "And in the South, when someone does something nice for you, it's customary to say 'Thank you.'"

"I am grateful. It's undeserved, but thank you." Elizabeth leaned against the metal doorframe of Tina's office. In her mid-sixties, Tina was pretty and round with curves in all the right places. She carried the robust air of a woman who worked hard and loved well. "Go, have fun with your grandkids."

"I'll text you some pictures. Cole and Haley have been planning this birthday party, for a five-year-old, mind you, for months. GiGi cannot miss. And Beth, a gift doesn't depend on merit."

Was there any place more humbling than Hearts Bend? Elizabeth had been raised to take pride in herself, her independence. But the folks of HB made trusting and leaning on others intoxicating.

"You know," Tina said, slinging her handbag over her shoulder, "I love Ella's. The ole girl was dying when I took it over twenty plus years ago. But I'm not married to the idea of going on forever and ever. Life's too short to be weighed down with that kind of pressure and worry, with so much focus on achievements and acquisition. Those things truly don't make us happy. Not long-term, anyway. Family is what matters. People matter. Faith matters. What we do with our time, money, and words matters."

Elizabeth listened because she respected Tina. The

woman had endured some trials in her life and raised three boys alone. She defined strength. Understood independence.

"Well, that's enough of a lecture." But it wasn't really. Tina walked with Elizabeth to the service window. "Oh, hey, when you close tonight, stick all the money in the safe. I'll tally it up in the morning."

"I'll do it, Tina. It's my job." Elizabeth reviewed the orders on the screen, then garnished a plate with coleslaw and a pickle.

"But you're already working when you should be, I don't know, out on a date with a gorgeous man. Oh, to be young again." She made a face, and Elizabeth laughed. "You are keeping your eye out for a young man, aren't you?"

"Absolutely not." Elizabeth turned toward the grill. "Shiloh, I need two number ones medium, and a number three grilled."

"Don't think I won't ask that question again, my little chickadee." Tina leaned against the counter. "You know, I always thought you'd take Ella's to the next level if you wanted."

"Ha, very funny, Tina. I have plans, and they don't include hot kitchens and greasy fry vats."

"Honey, I have people to clean the vats. I'm only saying—"

"You want me to forget my plans to fulfill yours. I thought you just said this place doesn't matter. It's people, family and friends."

"Exactly. Your people are here." Spotting the UPS truck, Tina moved around Elizabeth for the back door. After thanking the driver, she asked Cade to move the boxes to the storeroom, then returned to the service window, taking up the conversation where she left off. "I see how you fit into this place, even after being gone for so long. I don't want you to forget your plans. I want you to change them."

Was she serious? Elizabeth's plans had been formulated since eighth grade. "Nothing doing. I'm getting my MBA, then working for a Fortune 100."

"And then what?"

"Buy a stunning penthouse house, my dream car, and vacation in the South Pacific." Elizabeth garnished two more plates and notified the servers.

"By yourself?"

Elizabeth faced Tina, hand on her hip. "Oh, *okay*, I'll take you with me."

Tina laughed. "Fine, smart aleck. I'm only pointing out the obvious." She headed to the back door with a wave to the kitchen crew—Shiloh on the grill. D'Angelo on the fry vats. Cade on the dishwasher and every other odd job the kitchen required. Lucy supervised five other servers along with three busboys. "All right, my darlings, I'm out. Behave yourselves."

Head down, Elizabeth kept the orders going, garnishing plates and working the milkshake machine when the servers got backed up. Lucy reported the benches out front were loaded with folks waiting for a table or booth. Even the counter was full.

"Don't people in Hearts Bend have their own kitchens?" Elizabeth said.

"Not when Buck Mathews is singing in the park," Lucy said. "What a great town we live in. Country music singers, pro football players, an honest-to-goodness prince and princess. It's enough to believe in fairy tales."

"I believe in hard work." Elizabeth pointed to Lucy's plate under the heat lamp.

The night ran smoothly considering the non-stop table turnover. Every time the door opened, Elizabeth could hear the familiar melodies of Buck Mathews, Hearts Bend's own country music sensation. She'd met him as an up-and-comer when she waitressed at Ella's during high school summers.

"Elizabeth, the guy at the counter asked to see the manager." Lucy stood at the service window and pointed behind her.

"Did he say why?" Elizabeth fixed an order and shoved it under a heat lamp and paged the server.

"No, just that he wanted to speak to the manager, especially if she's the curly-haired brunette working the window."

"Very funny. He did not say that, Lucy. Is he a creep? A weirdo?"

"No, he's gorgeous. One of the WMA officers. His name is Ryder or something—"

Ryder. Elizabeth snapped her attention to the dining room. Ryder Donovan was here? She felt a bit wobbly when she spied him sitting on a counter stool. She casually checked her appearance in the stainless steel shake machine as she removed her gloves and, with a deep breath, headed through the double doors.

"Um, hello, Ryder?" she said, sounding more girlish than she wanted.

He looked up, then slid off the stool to stand in front of her. "Elizabeth? Hey, wow, look at you." His smooth baritone stirred feelings she'd forgotten. "It's been a month of Sundays, but...what are you doing in town?"

"Working. Here and Dorsey. I'm, um, taking a break..." From what? Suddenly, she couldn't remember why she was in town, because the spark in Ryder's chocolate-brown eyes made her forget she'd ever wanted anything but him.

2

He was joking when he mentioned the curly-haired girl to Lucy, never imagining Elizabeth Dorsey would be at Ella's Diner.

Seeing her erased the tension from his confrontation with Travis. First, the man accused him of hiring the loggers without a contract. Ryder knew nothing of it. Then of ordering a hundred and seventy-five feet of cherrywood to restore the old fire tower. Was he crazy? His initial order for the tower was pine.

But sure enough, his name was on the invoice. He had no recourse but to deny it.

"Are you back in Hearts Bend?" Elizabeth said. "I thought you worked out west."

"I was...out west. I came back." He remembered Elizabeth as brilliant and ambitious with a clear view of her future. And beautiful. Always beautiful. Even under that Ella's hat. "So, what are you doing here?"

"Another summer gig, if you can believe it. Working

at Dorsey during the day, and Ella's at night. I'm heading to the Wharton School in the fall."

"Wharton? Good for you. I knew you'd get what you wanted."

"Never doubt." Her smile lacked a bit of light, which made him curious.

But wow, it was good to see her. How many Saturday nights did he sit at this very counter waiting for her to get off work? Then go to her grandparents' basement to watch a movie, eating Ella's burgers and falling asleep on either end of the sofa. Summer after summer, they stayed in the friend zone. Then the year she headed to college, the Dorseys threw her a going-away party, and when he danced with her under the outdoor lights, his pulse was a runaway train. All he wanted to do was to kiss her.

"Lucy said you wanted to see me?"

"Right, I did. Yes." He pulled out of the past into the present. "An order I placed last week was canceled." He showed her the receipt. "I'd like to place it again. It seems that the TWRA can't afford a few chicken baskets with kids' toys."

Elizabeth's fingers brushed his when she reached for the order form. "Does the TWRA need a few chicken baskets with kids' toys?"

"I teach fire and wildlife safety at the Kids Theater. Food is a great enticement."

"And our tax dollars won't pay for it?"

Ryder tapped the order form. "Apparently not. Tina even gives us a huge discount."

"This sounds like politics."

She had no idea. "I'd like to reorder these, please. Pay out of pocket."

"Ah, the riches of the humble park ranger." She laughed softly, a slight blush on her cheeks. "I'll put this in for you."

"Here you go, Beth." Ryder turned to see Jeff Simmons, Elizabeth's cousin, walking toward them from the front door, jiggling a set of keys. "Four new tires with a spare in the trunk. You got the Tina Danner discount."

"More than a discount." Elizabeth reached for her keys. "She's paying for them."

"Yeah, well, Marty's still trying to marry her, so my guess is she'll never see that bill. Hey, Ryder, what's up?" Jeff slapped hands with Ryder, the WMA officer, who actually had more authority in this town than Jeff.

"Ordering food for the kids tomorrow." He glanced at Elizabeth and tripped into her sky-colored eyes. "Catching up with your cousin here."

"Don't get too close. She's leaving in the fall."

"Yeah, she said her plans were in play," Ryder said. "Headed to the Wharton School."

"Don't be jealous, boys. I'll remember you all when I'm sitting in my executive boardroom, running a Fortune 100 company."

"I'm sure Granny won't let you forget," Jeff said. "Hey, Beth, can I get a burger plate to go?" He pulled out a money clip and handed over a twenty.

As she waved Lucy over to take the order, Ryder looked and listened in as she chatted with Jeff about her new tires, shades of his younger, more carefree days, cooling his ire with Travis.

"Did I need four new ones? I've only had the car a couple of months."

"Your parents got ripped off with whatever tires they bought. You needed them."

"Is Tina now obligated to marry Marty?" The best mechanic in Hearts Bend had been after Tina Danner for as long as Elizabeth could remember.

Jeff laughed. "Tina's not marrying anyone she doesn't want to marry."

Ryder half listened and half drifted down memory lane to the summer nights they played volleyball or dodgeball on the Dorsey property, Pops Dorsey grilling out, hosting guitar pulls with Buck Mathews before he got super famous. It was the only time in Ryder's life he felt loved. Accepted.

The Dorseys were very different from his family. Ryder spent far too many lonely nights at the Donovan house, eating frozen dinners and playing video games.

"Hey, man, tell her." Jeff slapped Ryder's shoulder. "Tell her family helps family."

"Well, that's the general idea," Ryder said, his gaze crossing Elizabeth's. She knew a little bit about his teenage home situation, where family didn't always help family.

"Tina's not family," she said. "She's a friend. A good friend, but still—"

"Close enough," Jeff said, then responded to a call on his shoulder radio just as Lucy brought out his order. As he headed for the door, he pointed to Ryder. "Beth, have him tell you about the time he saved my life."

Ryder made a face. "He's exaggerating. I did not save his life. Back to my chicken basket order, I think I'd like to add a dozen boxes."

"Let me get Tina's iPad." Elizabeth disappeared

through the kitchen doors, returning a few moments later with the tablet.

"When do you need this?" He told her Thursday around four o'clock. She tapped on the screen, then handed him an Apple Pencil to sign on the bottom line.

"You're lucky, you know. To have a family who cares."

"I know," she said. "It's just odd. My dad was the only Dorsey to move away. I sometimes feel like I don't deserve all this familial affection. Then there were two years where I—" She smiled. "I should be more grateful. So, how are you?"

"Living the dream."

"Nice cliché."

He laughed. "I am. I always wanted to be a ranger."

"I remember. I think of you every time I see Smokey Bear."

"So, once, twice in the last seven years?"

"Actually, I went hiking six years ago in Colorado. I saw Smokey every day."

"So, what made you decide to leave the big Yankee city for luxurious Hearts Bend?"

"Getting some experience before Wharton working in Dorsey's financial office and moonlighting as a diner night manager. It'll give me some good stuff for my pre-exercise work going into my first term."

"Always the achiever."

"Yep, that's me." But her voice was strangely low and unconvincing. "Dad suggested Dorsey Furniture. 'It's a Fortune 10,000 company,' he said." Elizabeth glanced toward the kitchen. "I should get back to work, but it was good to see you. I'll make sure Tina has those chicken baskets ready for you tomorrow."

Ryder reached for her hand. "It was good to see you too."

As he exited the diner into Buck's country sounds, the warmth of her hand lingering in his, he tightened the strings around his heart. Beth's presence had loosened them. Still. After all these years. He'd have to be careful this summer, or he'd do something stupid and fall in love. As he made his way across the street toward the music-filled Gardenia Park, he couldn't help but glance back at the diner and, for one inhale and one exhale, imagine a future with the lovely curly-headed brunette.

———— ♥ ————

Of all her plans for the summer, running into Ryder Donovan was not one of them. His presence lingered with her the rest of the night.

Around nine thirty, as business began to wane, Elizabeth set aside thoughts of the handsome WMA agent and plopped down at Tina's desk with a large, icy tea, a plate of piping-hot fries, and a burger with no bun. In between bites, she worked through the receipts and tallied the tips. She counted the cash and punched the evening numbers into QuickBooks.

Her eyes burned from lack of sleep combined with the greasy kitchen air. Tina ran the best vent system in the business, but on nights like tonight, some of the hiss and sizzle lingered. She relished the idea of sleeping in tomorrow, but Tuesday morning was the all-hands meeting at Dorsey and a big day for the accounting department. In spare moments, she worked with the small marketing team Will had recently put together. She'd gain all the experience she could before grad school.

At ten, she locked the diner's front door, rolled up her sleeves, and broke down the kitchen with the rest of the crew, volunteering to finish mopping so Cade could clock out.

"Elizabeth, we're going over to the park. You should join us." Lucy paused by the fry vat, waiting for her boyfriend, D'Angelo, to finish cleaning up. He was the strong, silent type and a bull in the kitchen. "Buck's set is over, but some other folks play until midnight."

"I wish I could, but I have an early day tomorrow," Elizabeth said. "Good job tonight."

At her locker, she pulled out her backpack, checking her phone for messages. Granny had texted "Don't work too hard!" three hours ago.

She'd checked her Wharton application—just to see. No movement toward acceptance. She'd been to the campus, had a tour, sat in a class, joked with the admissions team. She felt sure she should have an acceptance letter by now.

Drained from the length of her day, she shut off the lights, locked the diner, and walked through the warm Tennessee evening toward her car—and its shiny new tires—with sounds of music rolling over the top of the diner.

Ten years ago, the town had still worn its old-fashioned ways with the downtown sidewalks rolling up at the proverbial five o'clock. Only the diner remained open. And a stroll down any Hearts Bend street had folks waving at you from their front porch.

But these days, with so much fame living in town—did she mention that Lauchtenland's Prince John and Princess Gemma had a home here?—Hearts Bend embraced more modern ways. The shops stayed open until nine. The park held a concert series year-round. All the while clinging to the good traditions of the past, like folks sitting on their stoops and waving to the neighbors.

She slowed as she approached her car. A man leaned against the hood of her VW. Elizabeth slipped her backpack from her shoulder, ready to swing.

"You're leaning on my car." The man jerked upright and swerved toward her. Ryder. She lowered her backpack with a loud exhale. "You scared me."

"Sorry. I saw you were still in the diner—" He moved toward her. "I thought I'd make sure you got in your car safely. This is your car, right?"

"Are you following me?" She tossed her backpack into the passenger seat. "I'll have you know my cousin is a Hearts Bend police officer."

"Yeah, well, I'm a TWRA agent with Cheatham WMA, which has way more authority than a local police officer. Also, I saved his life, so—" He shrugged and made a funny face.

Elizabeth laughed. "I think I need to hear this story."

"I don't know...if I tell you, then all the mystery will be gone, and what will we talk about over dinner?"

Smooth. Clever. He'd picked up some moves over the years. "Maybe," she said, trying to sound a bit mysterious herself.

Ryder had always fascinated her a bit. Two years older, a friend of her cousins, he'd never given her more than little-sister pat-on-the-head attention. Until the summer she was seventeen and they'd sat up all night on the high school bleachers talking about anything and everything. Oh, Pops had been so mad when she came home with the sunrise. Afterward, Ryder hung out with her almost every night, sitting on the back deck until the mosquitoes drove them to the basement to watch movies.

However, she wasn't seventeen anymore. She was twenty-five and three years behind in her life plan. Which meant romance must be pushed back three years, or more. Nothing for her heart until thirty-two or -three. Maybe thirty-four.

Yet this wasn't just any boy asking her to dinner. This was dark-haired, dark-eyed Ryder Donovan, who'd filled out his young-man skin and bones with muscle and might.

"Maybe?" Ryder said. "Is that a definitely maybe or a sort-of maybe. Perhaps a maybe, maybe?"

"More like a maybe-because-I-work-most-nights, but yeah, dinner might be nice." There. A nice, soft out. Noncommittal without rejecting him.

"I'll pencil that on my calendar. But for now..." He motioned to the park. "We could grab a spot on the green and listen to the last set."

"I would love to, really, but I'm exhausted, and I have to be at Dorsey Furniture by eight. Staff meeting at nine. Will doesn't believe in working remote. Yet."

"Then I'll say goodnight."

"Good night, Ryder, and hey, it was good to see you."

———— ♥ ————

On his back porch, with the sounds and scent of summer rising from the trees, Ryder eased into his oak rocker and popped the top from a bottle of water. He set the chair into motion while his German shepherds, Fred and Ginger, slept at his feet.

From his hilly perch off South Broad between Scott's Farm and the Cumberland River, the glow from the town center traced the treetops. He'd stayed for the last set in the park, keyed up from seeing Elizabeth.

On his way to his truck, he ran into country superstar Buck Mathews and his wife, JoJo, sitting on the tailgate of their truck, also listening to the last artist to play. They invited Ryder to join them and, for the next hour, chatted about life and love.

Buck won CMA Entertainer of the Year. Again. But he was really humble about it. The man simply loved making music.

Ryder never envied his friend's success. He appreciated that he stayed connected to his humble roots. Ryder had grown up with wealth and knew all too well it did not buy happiness.

What he envied in Buck was his marriage. The way JoJo looked at him. The way he checked with her as he told his stories. But when Buck leaned close and said, "Keep this to yourself for a day or two, but Jo's pregnant. Twins. We're announcing it this week," his heart unraveled with a bit of envy.

"Congratulations." He slapped Buck a high five and hugged JoJo.

A family. That's what he wanted. Ever since he was a kid. Then JoJo asked, in all sincerity, "What about you, Ryder? Anyone special? You're such a great guy, I can't believe no girl has snatched you up."

"Yeah, well, so far it's just me and the dogs up on the hill." No offense, Fred and Ginger.

"As I recall, you liked one of the Dorsey cousins," Buck said.

"That was a long time ago. And we were just friends." He glanced toward the diner, where Elizabeth had tilted his world a little. "But I'm open. You know anyone looking for a WMA officer to share her life?"

Buck laughed, but JoJo squeezed his hand. "She'll come, Ryder. She will. Have faith."

Have faith? That was his lifeline. And the hope he'd find someone to share the house he'd spent every waking minute and free dollar restoring. Someone to laugh with, to talk things over. Someone to love and give love.

In the end, all the talk of love made him restless. And Ryder didn't like being restless.

At his feet, the dogs stirred, reminding him he was home. "So, what'd y'all do today, Fred? Ginger?" It was down to this—talking to the dogs. "Jeff Simmons said I saved his life, but it's more like the other way around. I think he wanted me to look cool in front of his cousin."

The Dorsey clan had been the closest thing Ryder ever had to a real family. Then he went off to Vanderbilt, worked out west for a while, and let hometown relationships slip until he decided Hearts Bend was where he wanted to be.

He'd thought of reaching out to Jeff and other Dorsey folk in the past two years, but staying to himself had seemed safer. Easier.

"Your master is an idiot, Fred."

The big boy lifted his head with a single bark in protest. Not wanting to be left out, Ginger echoed. Ryder reached down to scratch behind her ears.

"You're my one and only girl, aren't you?" To which Fred responded by nosing Ryder's hand away from *his* girl. "Okay, Fred, I see how you roll."

He pulled out his phone and scrolled through his contacts, finding a seven-year-old number for Elizabeth Dorsey. Did it still work? Should he send her a message just to see? It was too late to call. While he wandered the land of indecision, his phone rang, igniting a barking frenzy. The screen displayed the goofy face of one of his Colorado ranger friends, Enzo Holder.

"You know it's after midnight here," he said.

"I figured it was my best chance of getting you to answer."

Ryder laughed. "What's up? Fred, Ginger, hush, it's okay. Lay down."

"How're Fred and Ginger?"

"Still in love."

"And your only companions?"

"Enzo, you did not call me up in the middle of the night to see if I had a love life."

"I'm hoping you don't. Skinner is leaving. I'm being promoted, and I want you to take my place. A lot of rangers remember your composure during the Grizzly Creek Fire."

Five years ago, the fire broke out in Glenwood

Canyon in August and took almost four months to get fully contained.

"So, you call in the dead of night, praise me for a past job, and think I'll say, 'Absolutely. You're offering me my dream job.'"

"That's one angle, yes."

Tempting. Ryder had loved the Aspen office of the White River National Forest. "I don't know, Enz. Hearts Bend is home. I feel like I just got here. I've remodeled my house. Everything is good except my boss trying to pin weird expenses on me. But it's nothing I can't handle."

"You're still an outsider, Ryder. He hired you, but he's putting you in your place. I've seen it before. I say quit. Come work for me."

Ryder rocked back in his chair, listening, as Enzo pitched the job.

"…great experience. All the skiing you can handle. Housing. Pathway to promotion. Promise me you'll think about it."

"I promise. Can you give me the summer?"

"You're killing me, Ryder, but yes, I'll give you the summer. Why? You think this boss of yours will suddenly like you?"

"Probably not, but there is—"

"A girl? I knew it. She's going to make my life difficult, isn't she?"

"I didn't even know she was in town, Enzo. I've not seen her in years. She used to come down in the summers, stay with family, and work at the local diner. I was friends with her cousins."

"Does she want to live in Colorado?"

"She wants to go to grad school in Pennsylvania."

"You think she's going to fall for you and give up her dreams?"

"More like I'd fall for her and give up mine. They need rangers in Pennsylvania, don't they?"

"No, I hear all those jobs are filled." Enzo laughed. "But hey, you promised to think about my offer. I'll be in touch."

When he hung up, Ryder collected the dogs and went inside. His place in the country was sort of a gift from his parents. Once they realized he wasn't going to law school with his eye on politics, they handed him the equivalent of four years' tuition at an Ivy League school and told him to use it for a house. Or investments. He'd spent almost half on this place and put the rest in the bank.

Flipping on the kitchen light, he retrieved last night's chicken cordon bleu from the fridge and warmed it in the air fryer. Growing up with workaholic parents, he learned to cook from the housekeeper and his Italian nanny. Besides the cordon bleu, he made a mean homemade ravioli.

So…Enzo wanted him back in Colorado? His "I want you here. I believe in you" was hard to resist.

The air fryer beeped. Ryder plated his dinner and headed for the living room. Sitting in the quiet, watching the stars peek through the skylights, he thought Elizabeth and her blue eyes were a far better sight than the Rockies of Colorado.

3

After a hectic week at Dorsey Furniture and Ella's Diner, Elizabeth treasured her Sunday morning sleep-ins. She started the day with a long soaking bath before heading to Java Jane's for a large latte and egg sandwich. Finding a cozy corner, she read the local newspaper—print edition—then read the news online, followed by the dozens of management, marketing, and finance articles that dropped into her inbox every week.

She'd developed this routine in college and held it sacred, especially after losing so much time being...ill. She'd never even heard of Epstein–Barr until the doctor's diagnosis.

However, in Hearts Bend, in Pops and Granny's place, Sunday morning was church time. This morning, like every Sunday morning, Pops sang hymns in the shower while Granny blasted worship songs from her kitchen speaker. Elizabeth burrowed under the covers and tried to sleep, waiting for the solitude to return.

On this particular Sunday, there was a knock on her door. "Bethy?" Granny said. "You awake?"

"I am if you want me to be." Elizabeth sat up, shoved her curls aside, and focused on the door as Granny peeked in. "What's up?"

She looked pretty in her periwinkle blue dress and white sneakers. In her late seventies, Granny kept up with the fashion trends while maintaining her grandma authority.

"You look tired," she said.

"Long week."

Granny sat on the edge of the bed. "You're allowed a day off, you know. Do you work at the diner tonight?"

"No. Tina told me not to go anywhere near Ella's."

"Good. You need a day to rest. You'll be in grad school in a few months, back to the grind. I know you're all healed up, but that virus can—"

"I'm careful, Granny, I promise. And I feel like I've rested enough for a lifetime. Sitting around feels like a waste of time, like my life is getting away from me again." There were days when she was too tired to lift her head and she wondered if she'd ever feel whole.

"Did you ever think life wants to show you something you're not looking for?"

"Those are what you call distractions, Granny," Elizabeth said. "If life throws something in front of you not pertinent to your plans, dreams, or goals, you kick it aside and keep moving forward."

"That doesn't sound very exciting," Granny said. "I do admire your ambition and how you've overcome adversity, Beth. The whole family is proud of you, but take it from an old gal, stop and smell a few roses now and then." She headed out, but paused at the door. "Pops and I would love for you to come to church with us this morning. It's one of the roses everyone needs to stop and inhale." She glanced at her watch. "Is thirty minutes enough time?"

You have to know something about Betty Dorsey. She was smart and kind with wisdom to spare. She loved well. Elizabeth never doubted her grandmother's affection for her. But when she said things like "Is thirty minutes enough time?" a girl moved. She wasn't asking a question.

Elizabeth slid out of bed for a quick shower, then dressed in white capri pants, a blue top, and her platform wedge sandals. Church was a big part of her summer memories, but not her life.

When Dad left Hearts Bend for college, he gave up on "religion." Mom claimed no religious affiliation either, so church never informed the Boston Dorseys' world, save the occasional Christmas and Easter service.

Slinging her bag over her shoulder, Elizabeth headed downstairs, wondering if Pops would stop at Java Jane's for a latte and egg sandwich on the way to church.

In the kitchen, Granny handed her a banana and said they were late.

"So, no Java Jane's?" Elizabeth said.

"Not before. After. I have a roast in the oven for lunch." And Granny was out the door after Pops, who wore black slacks with a blue shirt, his gray hair still thick and shiny. He'd been CEO of Dorsey Furniture until her cousin Will took the helm. But not before Pops brought the organization into the twenty-first century, even establishing an early partnership with the likes of Amazon.

Elizabeth planned to pick his brain before the end of summer. There's a thought—maybe attending church while waiting for the most important notification of her life had benefits. Like a smile from the Man upstairs. She decided to mention it to Him when the pastor had everyone bow their heads and close their eyes.

"Jeff said he saw Ryder Donovan at Ella's the other night." Pops glanced at Elizabeth through the rearview mirror as they passed the downtown shops and Java Jane's. "What was that about?"

"About Jeff making something out of nothing," Elizabeth said. "Ryder needed to order some kids' chicken baskets. That's all. He teaches fire safety or something."

"At the Kids Theater," Pops said. "I hear his boss is giving him a hard time. Travis can be a son of a gun."

"He mentioned the department isn't willing to pay for the baskets."

"Sounds like true love to me," Pops said with a low chuckle.

"Please, Pops, you're ridiculous." Still, their brief exchange outside of the diner popped into her head at odd times during the week. Staff meeting. Working the window at Ella's. Driving home. Now, while driving to church.

She couldn't remember when she met him. Ryder was always a part of her summer landscape. She'd friended him on Facebook and Instagram, but he rarely posted. Not much more than an annual photo of him fishing or hunting.

"I can still see you waiting in the living room for him

to pick you up for youth group." A grinning Granny looked back at Elizabeth. "You always looked so pretty."

"Well, I didn't want to look ugly." Youth group? She'd forgotten all about it. Those had been fun Sunday nights.

Pops turned into the church parking lot, and Elizabeth followed her grandparents toward the double doors and into the sanctuary, smiling and shaking hands as Granny said, "This is our granddaughter, Beth. Matt Jr.'s daughter. You remember her from working at Ella's in the summer."

Then there was the whole Dorsey crew to embrace: Ethan and his wife Julie; Will, handsome and single; Jeff and his girlfriend Ursula; Uncle Mac and Aunt Shell; Uncle Luke and Aunt Reece.

"We've got seats saved up front." Jeff hooked his arm around Elizabeth's shoulder. "How'd it go with Ryder?"

"How'd it go? He ordered kids' chicken baskets. End of story." She chose the last seat in the family row, just in case she felt like leaving early. The hallowed atmosphere felt strange to her. She preferred the hallowed halls of a university. That was her sanctuary.

As the rows filled up, she tried to remember if she'd enjoyed church as a teen. She had. Maybe? A few of Granny and Pops's friends recognized her and stopped to say hello. Then just as she started to relax, a masculine voice whispered over her shoulder.

"Is this seat taken?"

Finding Elizabeth in church was even more of a surprise than finding himself waking up early with a hankering for a holy place. Travis had been on him all week. Not just about expenses, but everything.

Did you get the brush cleared off Bramble Road?

I've not seen your environmental report. Are you going to do your job or not, Donovan?

Had the man hired him as some sort of scapegoat? Ryder worked late only to wake up early. He'd spent most of last week collecting soil samples and planting seedling trees, checking the lake and the docks. But he didn't mind. The forest was his sanctuary. His home. Yet this morning, he sensed a nudge toward the sanctuary of saints.

Then he saw Elizabeth and stopped mulling over how much he'd rather be in his kitchen stirring up homemade waffles with crushed pecans.

When he sat down, a soft note of her scent pulled him toward her. He tried to focus on the singing and preaching, but all he wanted to do was face Elizabeth, talk to her, reach for her, and step in close. Then, as the pastor finished up his message, he invited everyone to stand—God bless him—and hold hands.

Ryder looked at Elizabeth. She peeked at him. He offered his left hand while Jeff's girlfriend took his right. Elizabeth's soft palm slipped into his as the pastor prayed something about walking in the law of love instead of love of the law, but the drum of his pulse muted every other word. On the amen, Ursula let go, but Elizabeth held on for an extra moment or two. Or was he holding on to her?

"How were your chicken baskets?" she said, finally dropping his hand.

"The kids loved them."

"And learned only *they* could prevent forest fires."

He laughed. "Exactly. Especially in this dry, hot weather. We need rain."

Someone tapped him on the arm—Styles, a buddy from high school—and while Ryder slightly resented the interruption, he wasn't sure where to go next with Elizabeth.

By the time he finished reminiscing with Styles and meeting his wife and daughter, Elizabeth and most of the Dorseys had exited. But Granny D. caught him in the parking lot.

"Come to lunch. I've a pot roast in the oven."

"Are you sure?" Purely rhetorical. "No" was not an option with Granny D.

She made a face. "Of course I'm sure. Head on over, and no, you don't have to bring anything."

When the Dorsey crowd trailed off toward their cars, Ryder stood alone with Elizabeth. "Guess I'll see you at lunch."

"I guess you will." Her smile captured him.

Not good, Donovan. First of all, she was leaving in a couple of months. Second, he'd made an art form out of guarding his heart. Relationships caused pain. He'd learned that from his parents.

But then there was Elizabeth Dorsey. Somehow, she changed the game for him, and he wasn't sure he knew how to play.

Monday morning, Elizabeth woke early for an online Pilates class, trying to shake the sense of Ryder's hand in hers. But it clung to her skin, sinking in, causing her to want things a girl destined for Wharton should not want.

At Dorsey Furniture, her cousin Will met her in her office with an insurance payment snafu, so she spent most of the morning untangling those communication wires. And somewhere along the way, the feel of Ryder's firm palm finally began to fade.

"Beth, Court Chadwick just called." Will returned to her office after lunch. "He said you helped him with a payment plan. He's really, really grateful. He's pretty embarrassed about his company's financials, but you made him feel like everything was going to be all right."

"He's a nice man. I could tell he didn't like having to pay on installments. He'll be paid off by next summer."

"Dan also said you helped him out with a software issue."

Dan Cooper had been the CFO since Pops ran Dorsey Furniture. He was seasoned, wise, and a numbers whiz.

"I used the same program during an internship." Elizabeth stacked the folders she'd worked through that morning. "I can't believe they've not fixed that bug."

"Beth." Will leaned over her desk, propped on his hands. "Dan is retiring in three years. If you stayed here, you could work with him, learn the ropes of the business, take his place when he goes. Dan Cooper is a grad-school course walking."

"What? CFO?" She always thought she'd be a CFO by way of marketing and sales, maybe a few years in R&D, then leading a team on strategic initiatives. All corporate opportunities were excitingly endless. But to be a CFO before she turned thirty? And at Dorsey Furniture? In Hearts Bend, Tennessee?

"I know you have other plans, but please, think about it."

"You're serious?"

"Am I laughing? This is not nepotism. Okay, maybe a little. But I'd not offer you the job if I didn't think you could handle it. You're smart and talented, innovative. You're great with the customers and the employees."

"That's from my years of waitressing." Growing up, her parents had money, but they made it plain that Elizabeth did not. While they provided her needs, she provided her wants.

"And you put it to use. Not everyone does that, Beth. I've seen you with the staff," Will said. "They respect you."

"Because they think I'm leaving. Never mind bearing the Dorsey name."

"Believe me, they don't respect all Dorseys." He turned to leave, pausing at the door. "I had to go with my gut and make the offer. Let me know."

She sank slowly into the chair as Will made his way down the hall. What just happened?

Wait. No. She didn't have to think about it. Her future was not here. She didn't spend two years battling illness, propped on the couch, doing all she could to keep up with the world while too tired to lift her head, to join Dorsey Furniture.

Elizabeth sighed and glanced toward the window,

surprised by a rise of tears. What was wrong with her? Ever since church yesterday and holding Ryder's hand, and then the family dinner, her emotions sat near the surface.

Gathering herself, she chased Will to his office. "Hey, so are you officially—"

Just then, another Dorsey cousin, Ethan, looked in. "Jeff just called. They're looking for volunteers. A hiker reported gunshots near where Ryder Donovan was working. Now they can't get ahold of him."

"Let's go." Will fired out of his office with Ethan following. "Where? When?"

Elizabeth stared after them as their voices faded down the hall. Was Ryder shot? Who would shoot a WMA officer?

She jerked into motion and ran after her cousins, but they'd already disappeared down the steps and out the loading dock door. Back in her office, she texted Jeff, who never responded.

What should she do? She couldn't just stand here, waiting. But the Cheatham Wildlife Management Area was twenty thousand acres. Ryder could be anywhere. Bleeding. Dying. Alone.

She suddenly felt cold and reached for her sweater. He couldn't be out there *alone*. Dying. It wouldn't be fair after living most of his life alone, his parents off doing whatever they wanted, leaving him behind. Elizabeth may have had her issues with her parents over the years, but she'd never come home to an empty, dark house.

After a moment, she gathered herself and called Will. His voicemail answered.

"What's going on? Is Ryder all right? What happened?

Where are you? Call me!" She tossed her phone onto her desk.

Ryder exited her life the summer she left for college. She rarely thought of him. Even when she was sick and dramatically wondered if her life was over. Now she worried about him, sensing something wild and strange. As if losing him would cost her something very dear.

Like…her future.

Elizabeth launched to her feet and paced around her desk, then down the hall to the soda machine, where she punched the button for a root beer. Dorsey provided free sodas, teas, and bottled water to employees. She popped the top and took a long drink. *Calm down. He'll be fine. Ryder is a smart guy.*

Back at her desk, she tried to work but kept picturing him from Sunday afternoon, sitting at Granny's long picnic table under the giant oak, everyone talking at once, passing plates, asking "Scoop me some green beans, will you?" or "Can you ladle on some gravy? More than that—I want my food to swim."

Ryder talked about hunting season with Ethan, Jeff, and Uncle Mac, debating the superiority of the bow hunter over one with a gun. He looked so handsome in his white button-down shirt and jeans, vintage Pumas, and his dark hair somehow accenting his bright brown eyes and high cheekbones. She'd been staring at him when he suddenly looked up, locked eyes with her, and smiled. She instantly looked away.

She startled when her phone pinged. Jeff. Answering her text.

> **Jeff**
> Don't know anything yet. Pray.

Pray? She had no grid for prayer, but this was for Ryder. "Help. Please." That was a prayer, right?

Okay, she had work to do. A girl aiming to work for a Fortune 100 company could not be so easily distracted. In the middle of reconciling accounts, she came across a late payment flag for the Cheatham WMA. Ryder's name was on the order.

Elizabeth scanned the invoice, glancing at the balance. Eight thousand four hundred eighty-four dollars for one hundred seventy-five board feet of cherrywood from the Dorsey Mill side of the company.

That was a lot of money. What was Cheatham WMA doing with cherrywood? What was Ryder doing? Just last week, he paid for chicken boxes out of his own pocket because his office canceled the order. But they approved this? Then didn't pay?

Never mind that this seemed like a lot of wood for Dorsey to produce. In her five weeks on the job, Elizabeth had learned Dorsey—a furniture company—also provided lumber to select customers, holdovers from the Dorsey Lumberyard days. Then Great-Grandpa had a vision for fine furniture and changed the family's destiny.

Clicking through Cheatham invoices—there weren't many until a few months ago—then suddenly, orders for cherry. All with Ryder's name. Elizabeth reached for the in-house phone to buzz Grant Hansen, the production floor manager.

"Grant, it's Elizabeth." The motors of the machinery

filled the background. "Do we mill lumber for Cheatham WMA?"

"On occasion. Maybe for a special repair or small construction project."

"Cherry?"

He laughed. "Not unless they're building a forest castle. They usually order basic pine or spruce. We reserve all our cherry for furniture."

"But recently we fulfilled a cherry order for Cheatham. To the tune of eight thousand dollars."

"Can't be."

"Yeah, three months ago. Eight thousand four hundred eighty-four dollars."

Grant let out a low whistle. "I'd have to sign off on that much going out. That's about a hundred seventy-five board feet. Is someone fixing up a floor? That'd be one nice floor. Who fulfilled the order?"

Elizabeth checked the invoice. "It doesn't say."

"Okay. Let me see what's going on."

Elizabeth hung up and printed out the invoice just in case. She didn't know Ryder well in recent years, but the guy she knew from before was not a thief. And if he was, he'd be smart enough not to sign his name.

4

When he came to, he was at the bottom of a small hill with pain searing through his limbs. The ground beneath him was a collection of forest growth, rocks, and tree roots.

With a deep breath, he tried to open his eyes. The slit of light he caught from between the dense stand of trees made his head throb. In his mind, he hollered for help.

Wanting to stay awake, he roused himself enough to sit against a tree and tried to remember what had happened.

—Fixing a fence on Wade Reed Road.

—Sounds of chainsaws.

—Yelling. Running. Tripping. Tumbling. A sharp pain in his shoulder.

"Okay, Donovan," he muttered, the words clinging to his dry lips. "How are you getting out of this?"

The Middle Tennessee humidity blanketed him, but he needed to move. He felt along his belt for his phone, but the holster was empty. His firearm was also missing.

He opened his eyes enough to spy his cell phone a few feet away and stretched toward it with his boot. Yet before he could maneuver it toward him, he passed out, waking up with soft rain dripping from tree leaves onto his face.

He reached for his phone again, brushing the edge with the toe of his shoe, but not enough to pull it toward him. Finally, he lunged forward, reaching for it, sending a searing pain down his arm. And his left knee hurt like the dickens. He started to dial HQ, but between the trees and the clouds, he had no service. And *where* was his firearm?

Not good. Few traveled Wade Reed Road. He tried to stand, hugging the tree for support. But his knees buckled.

"You got this." He'd been here before, hurt and alone.

Peeking through the trees, he gauged the direction of the sun and decided to hobble north, if possible, and toward the road.

Ten trees later, he was exhausted. Every part of him throbbed with pain. Inching into a clearing, he sank down to the soft grass, fell back, and closed his eyes.

This seemed like as good a place to die as any.

Why wasn't anyone sending her updates?

Finding a break in Ella's evening rush. Elizabeth checked her phone for the millionth time. No texts. No voice messages.

Tina leaned over her shoulder. "Jeff said he'd call you when they found him."

"I don't know what you're talking about." Elizabeth tucked her phone into her pocket. "I'm waiting for an email from Wharton."

"Come on, I know a worried-about-the-boy-I-like look over an email-from-my-college look."

"First of all, it's not—" Never mind. She didn't want to tell people she was wait-listed. It felt like a negative confession. "I don't like any boy, Tina. But if you mean I'm worried about a friend lost, possibly shot, in Cheatham WMA, then yes, I'm hoping Jeff will call."

"Hmmm, tell me, when did you move to Denialville?" Tina carried a tray of clean glasses out to the drink station. "Hey Lucy, did you get the tables ready for the party of fifteen? They called. Said they were on their way."

Denialville? Tina thought she was so clever. Well, if anyone lived in Realville, it was Elizabeth Dorsey. She understood how life could upend a person at any moment. Therefore, nothing, *nothing*, not even a handsome ranger, could deter her. If any curveballs were coming her way, she'd be in the batter's box, bat raised, ready to swing. She'd had enough derailment for her twenty-five years.

For a Monday night, the dinner rush started late and ended early. By eight o'clock, she let two kitchen crew members go after cleaning and shutting down one of the grills and fry vats.

At nine, she sent two servers and one busser home. Tina came out of the office with a bag of laundry and her handbag.

"I'm dropping these at the dry cleaner, then home to a luxurious hot soak in my deep, luxurious tub."

"By way of Marty's Garage? See what he's up to?" Teasing Tina about Marty had become a thing between them.

"Marty's? What are you implying?" But there was a saucy grin on her lips. "Keep it up and I'll dock the cost of the tires from your check."

When he sent the bill for Elizabeth's tires, he'd charged her his cost and no labor. And there was a little tiny heart by his signature.

"Now who's living in Denialville, Tina? Huh?" Elizabeth laughed as her boss and friend flashed her palm and walked away.

"I'd fire you if I didn't love you so much! And I need you Fourth of July weekend."

The Fourth was a big deal in Hearts Bend. People came from all over to attend the celebration on Scott's Farm—now owned by the Castle family. Vendors applied months in advance to sell their art, craft, clothes, antiques, and, best of all, food. Local and Nashville music acts graced a giant stage with live music. There were games, bounce houses, and pony rides.

"Am I here or the farm?" Elizabeth said.

"I think I'll send you to the farm. I'm getting too old to stand in the heat and grill burgers. Lucy and D'Angelo can go with you. Okay, I'm leaving. Night all." Tina's voice faded as the door closed behind her.

So, Elizabeth would finally get to see the Fourth of July celebration. As a teen, she'd worked the diner while Tina and her sons manned the food truck at the farm. She, Lucy, and D'Angelo would make a good team. Even if those two were googly-eyed in love.

Look, she wasn't opposed to love. She was a red-blooded woman, after all. She believed relationships and commitment were an important part of being human. But she was three years off her planned goals, and if she didn't achieve them, she'd be a failure. Like she'd let Epstein–Barr win. The very idea made her anxious and out of sorts.

She was about to run the final evening tickets when there was a commotion from the dining room. Will and Jeff were moving toward the counter with a banged-up Ryder between them. He walked with a limp, and his arm was in a sling. Cuts and bruises marked his august face, and his hands were scratched and swollen, like he'd rolled through a briar patch.

"You found him." Elizabeth set aside the receipts and pushed through the kitchen door. "Thank goodness. Ryder, are you all right?"

"He ran into a tree chasing a couple of loggers," Jeff said, easing Ryder down on one of the counter stools.

"I didn't run into a tree." Ryder leaned over the counter until his forehead rested on the vintage Formica. "Food."

"We found him way out on Wade Reed Road. If he hadn't managed to get in a clearing, we'd still be looking." Jeff sat at the counter. "Can we get three burger platters?"

"Yes, of course." Elizabeth glanced at Will's somber expression. "Why isn't he at the hospital?"

"Just got back from there," Ryder said, his forehead still on the counter.

"He's got a slight concussion, banged-up knee and arm, bruises, and cuts. Nothing too serious. He's lucky."

"What happened?" Elizabeth said, punching in the order.

"Ryder's a bit fuzzy," Jeff said, "but remembers coming up on a couple of guys cutting down trees while mending a fence. He went after them but—"

"I did not run into a tree. There's a ravine. I went down it. *Then* I ran into a tree. Many trees. Lost my phone and sidearm." Ryder slowly sat up. The accident hadn't damaged his humor. "Where are we at on those burgers?"

"Coming up." Elizabeth poured tall glasses of sweet tea and water. "Are you sure you want a burger?"

"I've been dreaming of one all afternoon."

In the kitchen, she slapped the burgers on the grill and dropped a large basket of fries. Ryder was hurt. Then she dished out coleslaw and garnished the plates with spear pickles, lettuce, tomato, and onion. Ryder was hurt. She'd been more worried than she'd realized. Which she'd never confess to Tina. Ryder was hurt.

And he lived alone. Who would take care of him?

When she came around the kitchen door with their platters, Ryder whispered, "Thank you."

"How long were you out there? They said you were shot."

"I don't remember any gunfire. Too busy rolling down the ravine," he said, draining his glass in one long gulp. "I was out there about eight hours, and my ego is more damaged than my body."

"Someone was out there trying to illegally log trees," Jeff said, ending a call and setting down his phone with a nod of thanks to Elizabeth.

"They'll blame me," Ryder said. "My boss thinks I let loggers in without a contract. But I never talked to any loggers." He bit into his burger and slowly chewed. "My teeth hurt."

"An investigation will uncover the truth," Jeff said, then leaned toward Elizabeth. "Will told me he offered you the CFO job."

Ryder looked her way. "What? Another permanent Dorsey in town? Aren't we over our allotment?"

Will laughed. "She didn't say yes. Yet."

"I'm flattered, but that offer is outside my plan." She motioned to Ryder. "You guys should get him home. He's going to fall off his stool."

After the first bite, he never took another. She boxed up his dinner along with a dessert while Jeff cashed out with Lucy. Then she wiped down the counter and watched them go.

"You've got it bad for him," Lucy said as she collected the condiment bottles.

"I'm concerned for him. He was hurt."

"I think Tina's right. You've moved to Denialville."

"How can I deny something that's not true?" What was with small-town people who liked to be in everyone's business?

At ten, she locked the front door and turned off the lights. In the office, she tallied the receipts and worked up the deposit slip for Tina. She liked doing the extra things for a boss she admired.

"Everything's done. Cade is dumping out the mop water." Lucy leaned against the door. "Hey, Elizabeth, about Ryder. I'm just teasing. I really do admire your drive and determination. I wish I had it in me to go to a fancy college and get an MBA." She smiled softly. "But

I'm a country girl. I'm okay with attending UT and working here in the summers."

"If you're doing what you love, that's all that matters." Elizabeth tossed the money bag in the safe. "We're not all called to change the world the same way, Luce."

"I feel like I'm changing the world when someone walks into the diner, hankering for some good food, the best sweet tea in Tennessee, and a friendly face. Lonely, hurting people will never tell you they're lonely and hurting, but I can offer a smile and good service." She shrugged. "It's not getting into Wharton, but it's—"

"Something I should bear in mind," Elizabeth said. "You may do more for people than a thousand with an MBA."

"Will you visit when you're Miss MBA, working for some high-powered consulting firm?" Lucy said as they walked to their cars.

"Well, I might grace you with my presence." Elizabeth tried to sound light and confident. "If I'm not, say, in Tokyo presenting marketing strategies to Toyota."

"Sounds exciting." But Lucy didn't sound excited. Her reply felt more like placating Elizabeth. Because there she was jumping into D'Angelo's arms, who caught her up and swung her around before setting her down for a kiss. In the parking lot, he opened her car door, and while Elizabeth folded inside of her VW Bug, alone, Lucy drove away with a jolly toot of her horn, D'Angelo following in his truck.

Elizabeth spent her entire drive home arguing with herself about her life choices. They were just as valid as Lucy's or Jeff's, or Will's or cousin Ethan's, who headed up Dorsey Furniture's Business and Compliance Office and was married to a teacher, Julie.

Or Ryder, who returned to Hearts Bend to protect nature and wildlife.

Dad found love while getting his law degree. He had a family with Mom while building his career. While raising children and designing her dream home, Mom excelled as Director of Technology for a shipping company. They managed to chase their *dreams* and find love.

There was cousin Will, who didn't have a girlfriend but wanted one. His twin, Bobby, was married to Mila. Again, more Dorseys who found love and a career, right? There was no reason Elizabeth couldn't do the same. Two years of grad school wouldn't knock her out of the romance race.

Yet watching Lucy with D'Angelo—

"Let it go," she whispered to herself, shifting her car into gear. "You have plenty of time."

At home, the kitchen was bright and lively, cozy. Granny and Pops were at the table sharing their pre-bedtime toast and hot tea.

"Can I get you to join us?" Granny said.

"I'd rather have pie and coffee, but we can't do that anymore." Pops made a sad face. "Who invented heart-burn? I want to know."

Granny motioned for Elizabeth to sit. "Have you eaten? I made chicken and rice." She paused by the fridge, waiting for Elizabeth to answer, knowing full well it was one of her favorite dishes.

"A small bowl." She lowered her backpack to the kitchen floor. "Did you hear about Ryder? Jeff and Will brought him into the diner for something to eat, but he looked beat up."

"Yeah, Bill Yerkes from the TWRA headquarters called," Pops said between sips of tea. "They're having a real issue with armed loggers illegally cutting down trees."

"Is Ryder all right?" Granny said.

"Yes, but he's limping and his arm is in a sling. His face and hands are bruised and cut." Elizabeth twisted a paper napkin between her fingers. Why was this bothering her so much? "When Ethan first told Will, he said Ryder had been shot."

"I heard," Pops said. "Ryder's a smart officer. Experienced. He knows what he's doing." He tapped Elizabeth on the hand. "Did Will tell you he reserved our spot on Scott's Farm for the Fourth? The Dorseys are defending our three-legged race title."

"We could use you on our team." Granny warmed the chicken and rice on her old gas stove. "Beka is seven months pregnant, so she can't race." Beka was a cousin-in-law, married to cousin Chuck Dorsey.

"I'm working the diner's truck."

"At least you'll be there this year," Granny said. "You always worked at the diner before. Maybe you can take a break, walk around, and see the booths and games. I heard Buck Mathews is bringing a special guest. I hope it's Blake Shelton."

Pops's face made Elizabeth laugh. "She's got a thing for that Shelton boy."

"Matt Dorsey, I only have a thing for you. I just like Blake's singing."

"She never missed a season of *The Voice* until he left

the show." Pops pushed away from the table. "Betty, I'm headed up, otherwise I won't make that five a.m. men's prayer meeting in the morning." He kissed her good night and patted Elizabeth on the head. "It's good to have you here, Beth. We wish you'd never leave."

"Matt, don't start. We're supporting her educational pursuits." Granny set down a steaming bowl of chicken and rice in front of Elizabeth. "When you're ready for love, find a man like your grandpa. Though I'm not sure they make them like him anymore."

"Granny." Elizabeth stirred the chicken, rice, and gravy. "Do you really believe all this stuff about God? Does He really care? I mean, does Pops getting up for five a.m. prayer meetings make a difference? What's the reward? Does anything really change?"

"Elizabeth." Granny sat in Pops's chair, across from her. "Do you think your Pops is a smart man? A good man?"

"Absolutely. He brought Dorsey Furniture into the twenty-first century. He's a leader in the community. If I found a man like him, I'd be pretty lucky."

"Do you think he'd give time and energy to something that wasn't real?"

"No, but a lot of smart people do. We all have our blind spots." Elizabeth's first bite of chicken and rice warmed away all her inner angst about school, Ryder, and love. And the fact that she, too, had blind spots. She just didn't know where.

"We do. Which is exactly why Pops goes to those meetings."

Elizabeth made a face. "To find his blind spots?"

"Your grandpa decided long ago to be a man of faith.

So he gave himself to it. Just like he gave himself to our family, to Dorsey Furniture, and to exercising, but heaven knows he's let that one slide."

Elizabeth laughed. "When I was here in the summers, he always tried to get me to go to the gym with him. 'You'll love it,' he said."

"Then he wrenched his back, and that was all she wrote. But faith is something we all have to work out, Beth. Everyone believes in something or someone. Their education and intellect. Crystals and potions. Astrology. Nature. Their own strength and will. Even one's family can be a form of faith, I suppose." Granny pressed her hand on Elizabeth's. "But seeking the God who made it all? Who loves you even though He sees all your blind spots? That's one journey you won't regret. Not in this life or the next."

"I have faith, Granny. To succeed at Wharton, graduate top of my class with offers from top consulting or marketing firms, and—" Elizabeth glanced at her pinging phone. Her smile faded as she read the message.

"Something the matter?" Granny said.

"Not at all." Elizabeth rose from the table, leaving half of her chicken and rice untouched. "I'm pretty tired." She kissed Granny's forehead. "See you in the morning."

"Beth, I'm your grandmother. I've seen that look of disappointment on your face a hundred times. When you dropped your ice cream cone, when you got tagged out at first base." Granny's soft hands held onto hers. "Something about school?"

"Yes, um…" If she looked into Granny's warm, brown eyes, she'd lose it and tell the truth—she'd been wait-listed. She wasn't going to Wharton in the fall unless something changed. Soon. So she stared at the floor. "The apartment I wanted fell through."

"Well, you'll find something soon. Talk to Mila. She knows a lot of people in Philly. She grew up there." Mila, Bobby's wife, had already traveled the educational road Elizabeth was on.

"I will. Don't know why I didn't think of it."

Because she'd break the moment Mila started asking questions. Or shared some grand, lovely story of her post-grad years. Or how exhilaratingly hard it was but oh so worth it.

She still had a few weeks. She'd make it. She always did. So don't worry, Elizabeth Dorsey. But the fact that she stood in the same kitchen, in the same town as seven years ago when she graduated from high school, made her feel stuck.

Storing her uneaten dinner in the fridge, she headed up to her room, thinking of Pops and Granny, wondering if she needed a little bit of their faith.

5

———————

His tumble down the hill relegated him to three days at home and a week of desk duty, answering phones, doling out fishing licenses. So when the Fourth of July rolled around, Ryder was more than ready for the celebration at Scott's Farm.

He moved slowly in the mornings, and today was no different. He showered and dressed, then ate a bowl of cereal at the kitchen counter. Beyond the windows, the July sun celebrated America's independence by burning away every last fluffy cloud.

Today should be fun. And he needed a distraction. Being stuck alone at home or at his desk stirred old feelings. Lonely feelings. Tina had kindly sent meals his way a couple of days—for which he was grateful—but never by Elizabeth. Of course, she worked during the day and—

Rein it in, Donovan. He'd thought of her entirely too much lately. That was the worst part of being cooped up at home with only Fred and Ginger to keep him company.

The second worst part was being on desk duty, sitting outside Travis's office, listening to his big voice glad-handing on the phone, talking to investigators about the illegal removal of trees, trying to blame "a member of my staff."

Ryder had a growing sense Travis wanted to pin recent messes on him. Which came first? The odd cherrywood orders or the loggers without a contract? Did they both point to him somehow?

Never mind. Today he was celebrating his country and his freedoms with good food, good music, and good friends. Maybe even try to dance with a pretty, curly-headed brunette. His cuts were healing, and the bruises, which got worse before better, were just beginning to fade. He did look like he'd gone a few rounds with Mike Tyson and lost.

He rinsed his bowl and set it in the dishwasher, then gently stretched his shoulder—which hurt, but the pain was bearable. Taking his keys from the hook by the kitchen door and grabbing the cane he used to keep pressure off his knee, he headed out.

At Scott's Farm, he crossed through the crowded and lively grounds, looking for the Dorsey family camped under a wide oak. He'd missed the event two years ago, busy moving. Then last year he'd worked. This year, being on injured reserve had at least one perk.

"Ryder! Just in time." Ethan grabbed him into the Dorsey family huddle. "We're dividing into teams for the three-legged race."

"Ethan," Granny D. said. "The man has a cane. He can't run."

"I don't know…I can give it a go." Ryder bounced around, but his knee buckled a little. "With the right partner." His gaze fell on twelve-year-old Austin, son of one of the Dorsey cousins. The kid smiled. Ryder smiled.

However, Austin was paired with someone else for the kids' division. Will made a team with Markey, yet another Dorsey cousin. When Ryder was younger, he desperately wanted to be a Dorsey cousin. They were everywhere.

Jeff and Ursula paired up, and Ethan and Julie. Pops and Granny signed up for the senior division. That left Ryder without a partner.

"I'll get Beth." Jeff backed toward the line of food trucks tucked under a row of shady trees. In the distance, the first band of the day warmed up on the bandstand. "She can break away for one run."

"Hey, that's okay. She doesn't have to—" But Jeff was already making his way down the row, calling for Elizabeth like she was lost in the woods. He rushed back, saying, "She's in. We'll get her when we need her."

Ryder hobbled with the family toward the section roped off for the three-legged race. Maybe he should back out. His knee was aching just from the short walk. Running injured risked further damage to his knee and shoulder. Falling might hurt Elizabeth or any team they tumbled into.

Yet he wanted to race. Wanted to test his mettle. Want to rope his leg with Elizabeth's and link his arm around her. Hooley, who still manned the race with his clipboard and bullhorn, marched into their midst.

"Okay, Dorseys," Hooley said. "Give me your teams. You know you ought to let some other folks win now and then. Did you hear about the year we had a prince in the race? Yeah, Prince John from Lauchtenland. That's how he met Gemma. She's a princess now. Go figure. But I guess all y'all know that, eh? So what you got for us, Dorseys?"

"Yes, we know all about the prince and princess, Hooley," Granny said. "We live here too, you know? And we've lost races to the Wedding Shop teams plenty." Granny D. looked over at Haley Danner and her husband Cole. "We're coming for you."

"Bring it on, Betty," Haley said, laughing.

"Say, Ryder, you back in town?" Hooley licked the tip of his pencil and jotted down his name. "Who you racing with, and what's your team name?"

"Elizabeth Dorsey. And um, well—"

"'And um well' ain't a name. How about D and D? Donovan and Dorsey."

"Team D and D?" Ryder made a face. "How about Team Winners?"

"Please," Hooley said with a scoff. "I get a dozen folks saying that to me every year."

"Losers?"

Hooley laughed. "Never heard that one before. You want me to write down *Losers*?" He poised his pencil over the clipboard with one eye on Ryder. "Don't blame me when you actually lose."

"Okay, okay, how about Forest Boy-City Girl?"

"Kinda long, but I like it." Hooley wrote it down, running out of room at the edge of the page. "Got a ring to it."

To be honest, Ryder wasn't sure Elizabeth would even show up. She was dedicated to her work and, frankly, didn't like being told what to do.

But when Heat Seven was on deck with Hooley shouting, "Forest Boy-City Girl," Elizabeth ran up beside him.

"Hey," she said, the high planes of her face shaded by her Ella's Diner hat. "Did Hooley come up with that name or you?"

"He wanted D and D." Ryder handed Elizabeth the burlap bag, then stooped to tie their ankles together. "I'm tying you to my banged-up knee. If you can help hold me up, I'll try to carry more weight on my outside foot."

"Don't worry, Donovan, I can hold you up." He caught her grin, and he tripped a little further down the I've-got-a-crush-on-you trail.

They tested the strength of his tie, then dunked their legs into the sack. Try as she might to take the pressure off his knee, Ryder still had to add weight. The ache was turning into a gripping pain.

After a couple of practice runs, Hooley called Heat Seven to the starting line.

"Wrap your arm around me tight," Ryder said, slipping his arm around Elizabeth's waist. He tried not to think about being so close to her or how the curve of her waist felt under his hand, but her subtle scent—soap, perfume, and a hint of…chocolate?—refused to let him go. In all the days and nights they'd hung out together, he'd never managed to get this close.

"Y'all racers, ready?" Hooley stepped up to the sideline with his bullhorn. "On your mark, get set…"

At the starter pistol, Ryder and Elizabeth jumped out

to an early lead, but after a few yards, they lost their rhythm.

"Ryder, we're going to fall."

"No, we're not. Slow down for a sec…inside legs, outside, inside, outside." And they were off again, his knee protesting with every move.

The couple next to them tripped and fell in their path. Elizabeth muttered, "Jump," as they kicked over them. Ryder's knee buckled, but he wasn't going to quit now.

They hurdled another couple who'd fallen, landing a bit awkwardly on their joined legs. Ryder breathed through a sharp pain slicing through his leg.

To their left, Ethan and Julie raced with skill. Ethan had been a star athlete at Rock Mill High. On their right, Will and Markey were laughing so hard they kept falling and getting back up.

To his surprise, he and Elizabeth were in third place as they rounded the tree and headed back toward the finish line. Elizabeth's expression was focused as she whispered, "One, two, one, two."

In a single moment, he saw her, understood her. She was focused. Driven. Determined. Once she grasped an idea, she owned it. She'd achieve what she wanted in life. And it probably didn't include being married to a state wildlife officer.

"Oh my goodness, I think we're going to win." Elizabeth shot him a sideways glance, her expression so bright he could see nothing else.

"Move over Forest Boy and City Girl." Crud. Ethan and Julie were right on their tail.

"No way, Ethan!" Elizabeth steered toward the middle of the track to cut them off. The girl wanted this.

Without a word, Ryder gripped Elizabeth tighter and picked up the pace. Except his knee was done. He pushed harder, but right at the finish line, his leg buckled, launching him and Elizabeth face-first onto the mowed ground. They tumbled and rolled, stopping with their noses inches, *inches*, from the finish line.

"We can't even win by a nose," Elizabeth said, her laugh muffled by the grass.

"I'm sorry. My knee gave out."

"What?" She struggled to sit up, shoving their joined leg from the gunny sack. "Let me see." She pulled away the rope and inspected his knee as it peeked out from the hem of his shorts. "Hey, can we get some help over here?"

"Elizabeth, shhh, it's okay, I can get up." But Jeff and Will were already hoisting him off the ground.

"Let's get him to the medical tent."

"Stop, stop." Ryder pulled away from them. "I'm fine. Just give me a sec…" He hobbled off, embarrassed he'd let his ego shove away good friends. Embarrassed his ego had gotten him in the race in the first place. He was such a sucker for family. For Elizabeth Dorsey.

He found a knoll near the river and sat, the air off the water cooling his warm skin. Rubbing his knee, he kept his gaze away from the race site, hoping the Dorseys' attention had moved on to the next heat.

"We almost had it." Elizabeth plopped down next to him. "Stupid hole. That's why we fell."

Ryder laughed softly. "You're a terrible liar, Beth. My knee gave out, and we both know it."

"And I hit a hole." She jutted out her leg to show her ankle. "See, it's red. A little."

He reached for her slender calf, pulling it to him for

inspection. But the moment his hand touched her skin, his knee no longer seemed to be a source of bother. He set her foot down without looking over at her.

"Your ankle is fine. However, I should take you to Angelo's for pizza as a consolation prize."

"You don't owe me anything, Ryder," Elizabeth said, reaching to pick a dandelion rising between blades of grass.

"It's just pizza. Not resigning your independence or anything."

"I know, I know, but pizza is like...*the* classic date," she said. "Everyone will think that's what we're doing, sitting in the romantic candlelight of Angelo's, standards playing on the jukebox, sipping sodas and eating garlic roll appetizers."

"Sipping soda and eating garlic rolls. I said pizza. You want a soda and garlic rolls, you're on your own."

She grinned and tossed her dandelion at him. "Fine. Pizza. But it's not a date."

"Absolutely. Consolation prize only. Why would I want to date you?"

"More like why would I want to date you?"

She smiled and bumped his good shoulder, but she'd hit on a subtle truth. Why would this gorgeous, smart, ambitious woman with nice ankles—though one *was* slightly red—want to be with him?

"How's Monday night?" she said, helping him to stand. "I have the night off from Ella's."

"Six o'clock? I'll pick you—"

"I'll meet you there," she countered. "And make it six thirty."

6

All day Monday, the anticipated pizza date-but-not-really-a-date with Ryder proved to be a distraction.

Will asked Elizabeth for the week's receivables, and she delivered last year's. When the phone rang, she answered, "Ella's Diner," and during the afternoon marketing meeting, she kept drifting off, staring out the window.

Was pizza at Angelo's a date? It felt like a date. Rather, she *wanted* it to be a date. She still remembered how her hand felt in his that one Sunday morning. How his hand tight around her waist made her feel like she was his. How his touch sent a thrill through her when he examined her ankle.

Late Monday afternoon, Will entered her office and sat. "What's up with you today?"

She gave him her surprised look. "Nothing. Typical day."

"Anything bothering you?"

67

Part of her wanted to come clean and confess *I think I have a date with Ryder, but we're calling it a consolation prize.* But the confession sounded so benign. Who cared about one date when she was leaving in six weeks? Her imagination was making too much of this pizza dinner.

"Does your distraction today have anything to do with tonight?" He sounded like her big brother-cousin. The one who cared for her. "Pizza with Ryder?"

"You know?" She sat back with a sigh. "What is with this family? Everyone knows everyone else's business."

"We look out for each other, support each other, and cheer each other on."

"I'm not used to it, that's all." Elizabeth shuffled papers around, keeping her gaze averted. Will's piercing eyes made her feel vulnerable, as if he could read her thoughts. "Mom and Dad raised Jonathan and me to be independent and self-reliant."

"Don't kid yourself. Pops and Granny raised all the Dorsey kids to be independent and self-reliant. Where do you think your parents got the idea? But they also raised us to care for each other, to be friends as well as family."

"That's well and good, but aren't some things in life private and personal?"

"Yes, but some are meant to be celebrated." Will headed for the door. "Maybe you don't want people to know because you're hiding, Beth. Not from us, but from life's options. You think the only choice for you is education and a Fortune 100 company. But what if the best for you is here, in Hearts Bend, with the family, with Ryder Donovan?"

"Oh, really? Why don't you just say what's on your mind, Will?"

"I think I just did."

———— ♥ ————

"He's in one of his moods," Cheryl warned, nodding to Travis's office, her eyes heavy with longer and thicker false eyelashes.

Ryder sighed. He'd woken up with a weak and throbbing knee—the race had been foolish—but his consolation, non-date pizza with Elizabeth tonight, eased a bit of the pain.

His nine a.m. appointment with his doctor went well. Yes, he'd given him the stink eye for running a three-legged race, but he'd predicted the knee's full recovery and given him a shot of cortisone. Next week, he could return to regular duty if he took it easy.

Ryder planned to approach Travis about the fire tower refurbishment. He could do that without stressing his wounds.

"What's triggered him this time?" he said to Cheryl, setting his water bottle on his desk adjacent to hers. Travis's mood had been even more temperamental lately. He came in late. Worked behind the closed door. Scrutinized everything and everyone.

"I have no idea," Cheryl said.

Leaning on his cane, Ryder hobbled to Travis's office door, knocked, then peeked inside. "You wanted to see me?"

The large man jerked with irritation. "The refurbishment budget. What are you buying, Donovan, gold-plated screws and platinum nails?"

"No, sir." He hadn't done anything with the project in weeks. Since ordering the original pine and hardware. "You know what I ordered. I showed you the invoice."

Travis leaned toward Ryder with narrowed, mud-brown eyes. "I'm getting heat from accounting. This is taxpayer money you're spending, Donovan."

"I'm not spending it."

"Well, it's charged to your refurbishment account." Travis read from a printed-out report. "Cherrywood?"

"I ordered pine boards, which are still in my work shed." Ryder hated being on the defensive.

"Not according to accounting's records." Travis rose to his feet and placed a hand on his thick hip. "Tell me now. Are you the one behind this illegal logging gang? We didn't have this problem until you showed up."

"Illegal logging...?" His skin burned under his collar. "No. And why don't you tell me what this is really about?"

"Havoc in my department." Travis pounded the desk. "Out-of-control spending. Losing valuable forest to chainsaws."

"If you're accusing me, then form an investigation. I'll be happy to clear my name." The job offer from Enzo paraded across his mind with great appeal.

"I'm not accusing you of anything. Yet," Travis said. "But I'm up for promotion, and I won't have my career toppled by you."

"And I won't have mine toppled by you."

Back at his desk, Ryder dropped into his seat, his knee aching like a banshee.

Cheryl sashayed over. "I told you he was in a mood."

After a moment, Ryder grabbed his keys, headed for his truck, and drove out of town. What was going on? Travis had been the reason he returned to Tennessee and the Cheatham WMA. Now the man treated him like the enemy.

Down River Road toward Wade Reed and the dilapidated fire tower, Ryder shook off the conversation with Travis. The tension of the argument eased a little as he gingerly made his way up the tower's rickety stairs, careful of the weather-worn boards. Someone was messing with the department's finances. With illegal logging. And trying to pin it on him.

♥

Will had some nerve, didn't he? Suggesting she'd discover the best for herself in Hearts Bend? With the family. With Ryder. Which was crazy. He'd not so much as romantically held her hand or kissed her. He was nothing more than a good friend.

She reached for her phone a half dozen times to cancel the pizza not-a-date dinner. When she chickened out of that, she called Tina to see if she needed help at the diner.

No! Go to pizza with Ryder. Have fun, girl. You're young.

Go to pizza with Ryder? Did the whole town know? Was it in the Monday paper or posted on the Gardenia Park bulletin board? Will's comment about celebrations sat at her mental table. *Some things are meant to be celebrated.*

True. And nearly winning a heat in the Fourth of July three-legged race was toast-worthy. But who was she kidding? Tonight was about more than pizza with a friend. She felt it—the beginning of something lovely that, if she gave in, could overtake her.

She started when her phone rang. It was Ryder. "I've been thinking," he said. "Maybe we should cancel tonight."

——— ♥ ———

Ryder scanned the panoramic view of lush green trees and rolling hills from atop the fire tower, waiting for Elizabeth's response. Yes, he was worked up over Travis's accusations, but that's not what caused him to conclude Elizabeth wasn't all that excited to join him at Angelo's.

"Oh," she said, a hint of a question in her voice. "I-I was sort of wondering the same thing. You think we should?"

"Do you? I think I talked you into pizza. You're too nice to say no." He raised his binoculars to check for signs of smoke. Among the green, he spied patches of dried, fallen limbs among dried brush. With another week of no rain, the WMA really needed to issue a fire ban.

"Give me credit, Ryder. I know how to say no." The question in her voice turned to a lilt. "Will said something this afternoon about celebrating. And even an almost-win is worth celebrating."

"He makes a good point."

She sighed. "If I sounded like I didn't want to go, I'm

sorry. It's just I'm not used to everyone knowing my business. Not used to a social life. I'm so behind in school, and I feel like if I don't go to grad school and get that MBA, I'll regret it as long as I live. This is one of those do-it-now-or-do-it-never moments. Being sick—"

"You were sick?"

"Yeah, I was. For over two years. I don't really like to talk about it. Anyway…you'd better not back out on me on pizza. I skipped lunch to be ready for garlic rolls, soda, and all the pizza I can eat."

"Two years is a long time, Elizabeth. Are you doing okay?"

"I am. I just can't overdo it. And remember the part where I said I don't like to talk about it?"

Yeah, he'd heard, but that wasn't good enough for him. He wanted to know everything about her—from her favorite color to her pet peeves to how she'd recovered and graduated from MIT with honors.

"Can I say you look beautiful and healthy?"

"All day, every day."

Gladly. Ryder loved the laugh in her voice. "So, are we canceling tonight?"

"One does have to eat, and Granny doesn't cook on Monday nights. She claims she has to recover from Sunday's family dinner."

"No one does Sunday dinner like Granny D. If we go to Angelo's, we can order tiramisu."

"I love tiramisu."

"Then see you at six?"

"Six thirty," she said. "Hey, Ryder, where are you? I hear birds."

"At the old fire tower. Travis was…Never mind. I'll

see you tonight." He felt dumb enough calling to cancel. He wasn't going to whine to lovely Elizabeth—who'd battled illness for over two years—about his boss.

A warm breeze whistled through the broken boards of the tower, and Ryder vowed to give it all the love he could muster. Because broken things always needed love.

———— ♥ ————

As Elizabeth got ready that evening, Granny fussed around Elizabeth's room, up and down the hallway, humming the same tune over and over as she pretended to organize the hall closet.

"It's no big deal, Granny. Just pizza," she called, digging her white flip-flops out from under a pile of shoes.

Granny peered inside. "Did you say something?"

Elizabeth laughed. "I know you're hanging around to see what I'm wearing." She glanced in the floor mirror, then at Granny. "Well?" She wore white shorts, a navy-blue tank top, and her hair scooped into a top knot with curly tendrils around her neck.

"You look beautiful," Granny said. "Can I give you some advice?"

Elizabeth pursed her lips and tipped her head to one side. "If I say no, will that stop you?"

"Doubtful." Granny pulled out the desk chair and sat down. "Have fun, Beth."

"That's your advice?" Elizabeth searched her jewelry box for a pair of small blue diamond earrings. A gift from her brother Jonathan one Christmas. "Have fun?"

"You've been working sixty, seventy hours a week. It's okay to let go a little, exhale, see how the other half lives. You don't want to arrive at Wharton worn out. Your immune system is—"

"Fine, Granny. The virus isn't active."

"No, thank the Lord, but you can't wear yourself out."

"I won't, I promise. Pizza with Ryder is me having fun." Elizabeth sat on the bed across from Granny. She was so beautiful with her carefully combed silver hair and steady blue gaze. "I try not to be stoical and serious, but after being sick for so long…I should be graduated by now and at my first job."

"Beth," Granny said. "It's one thing to be sick. It's another to let it steer your decisions after you've healed. Use what happened to you as a reminder that life is short. We never know what's coming. Give yourself to the things you can take with you when you die."

"And what would that be, Granny?"

"How well you've loved others. What you've done with your time, words, and money."

"I try to do well with those things. It's just that—"

"Oh, Elizabeth." Granny hugged her close. "It's just that you hate to give up on a plan."

"Does that make me the bad guy? Inflexible?"

"No, it makes you determined. But don't forget the importance of love along the way. Now go." She turned Elizabeth toward the door. "Have fun tonight."

Elizabeth had just arrived at Angelo's when her phone pinged with a message from her friend Jordie.

Jordie
I got into Kellogg!! They took long enough to tell me. I was getting scared. But I'm in. If Wharton hadn't accepted you, I'd beg you to come with me to Evanston. We could've roomed together. How's it going in...where are you again?

Elizabeth
Congratulations! You're going to kill it. Yeah, Kellogg is a great school. I'm in Hearts Bend, TN. Working in the finance office of the family biz.

Jordie
Great experience! When do you leave for Philly?

Elizabeth
First of August.

She hated lying, but confessing she'd been wait-listed felt like defeat. She simply had to keep believing.

She jolted at a tap on her window. Ryder. Leaning down, peering in, a soft expression on his very fine face. Elizabeth popped open her door.

"Sorry, texting with a friend. She got into Kellogg." Elizabeth grabbed her bag, held her head high, and shut the car door with resolve. There was no need to tell Jordie, or anyone, the truth. Her good news would come any day now.

"Kellogg?" Ryder said. "Wow. I didn't know you could get an advanced degree in Special K, Cap'n Crunch, or Rice Krispies."

She laughed. "Really, yes, it's all the rage among the

Ivy League these days. And Cap'n Crunch is a Quaker Oats brand."

"Wow, so you really can get an advanced degree in cereals. Who knew?"

Just like that, Ryder Donovan eased her anxiety. Like he'd always done in days and summers past.

7

———————

All joking aside, Ryder suspected something about the text had upset Elizabeth. He saw it in the way she fumbled with her phone. How she averted her gaze when she stepped out of the car. Plus, he was raised by competitive people. He understood the world of achievers.

"Ready for some fun?" he said, holding open Angelo's door for her.

"It's the reason I came." But her smile lacked her usual brightness.

The hostess gave them a booth by the window and lit the candle in the middle of the table.

As they read the menu, he said, "Why'd the text bother you?"

"What?" Elizabeth glanced up, her eyes wide, reflecting the candlelight.

The server appeared for their order. "Sodas," Ryder said, checking with Elizabeth. "Garlic rolls and—"

"Large pepperoni and mushroom." Elizabeth handed her menu to the server. Then to Ryder. "I remember that was your favorite back in the day."

"I believe it was yours too."

She never answered his question, so he let it go and went with small talk—"How was your day?"—until the drinks and garlic rolls arrived.

After one roll, Elizabeth said, "I'm wait-listed at Wharton." She peered at him. "No one knows. Well, except you."

"I see. And your friend is headed to Kellogg." Now he understood why the text bothered her.

"I know her success doesn't make me a failure, but it feels like it."

"Who knows what goes on in admissions offices, Elizabeth. There are so many variables. Did they give a reason for wait-listing you?"

"They don't tell you. Even more puzzling, the notice arrived after I visited the campus and the admissions office. I thought for sure I was in, you know? They like the personal touch, but—" She tore a small piece from the garlic roll and popped it in her mouth. After a swig of soda, she sat back with a sigh. "I contracted Epstein–Barr my sophomore year at MIT. But I kept plowing ahead. Barely. I was exhausted, in my bed every free moment, sleeping. I had some pain and inflammation. By the summer, I was down twenty pounds, pale, weak, feverish. I thought I'd get better over the summer. I didn't. The doctors ran all kinds of tests, but nothing was conclusive." Her eyes glistened with tears. "Not knowing was worse than anything."

"So you were sidelined."

"For two years. Went to more doctors than I care to remember until one figured it out. The homeopathic doctor did a lot to help me recover my immune system, but the virus never goes away. So I'm told. And I was really scared. You read stuff online, and I had one foot in the grave." By the look on her face, she'd never said that out loud before. "I don't want to be scared, Ryder. I don't want to feel that fear, that helplessness, again."

"I'm surprised your granny isn't all over you about working so much."

"She is, but I'm careful. I take my supplements, but I need to eat better." She snatched another garlic roll. "But tonight is about fun, right? So here's looking at you, kid."

"And you." Ryder reached for a roll of his own. "My boss is on my case. Someone ordered a bunch of cherry-wood, and he thinks I'm using it to fix up the fire tower. Or maybe my own place, but I didn't order it. He's also alluding to me being behind the illegal loggers."

"So you threw yourself down a ravine to look inno-cent?" Elizabeth said.

"Yes, but don't tell." Ryder grinned.

"Seriously, what do you think is going on? There's nothing worse than being falsely accused." Elizabeth looked away, as if considering her next comment. "I wouldn't have said anything, but Ryder, your name is on an invoice at the shop for cherrywood."

"When? I couldn't have ordered it."

"The spring. Grant said they'd never cut cherry for the TWRA. It's used for fine furniture or flooring."

"I promise, Elizabeth, that order did not come from me." He shoved the last bit of the roll in his mouth. "I got a job offer in Colorado. Maybe I should go if—" He caught himself reasoning out loud.

"They'll really think you're guilty if you leave." Elizabeth sat back as the server set down their pizza. "Besides, you just moved here."

"Are you saying you'll miss me?" Ryder handed her a plate with a large slice.

"Well, no, I mean, yes, but it's not Hearts Bend without you." She bit into pepperoni, cheese, and sauce.

"Funny, I think it's not Hearts Bend without you."

What was happening? The romantic atmosphere of Angelo's, that's what. The candlelight, the soft glow, Dean Martin singing "That's Amore," and she's suddenly hinting to Ryder Donovan she'd miss him. Why did she care where he lived? Good luck to him.

"—not sure I can leave. Hearts Bend gets in your blood. Never mind my childhood." Ryder reached for another slice of pizza.

"I remember your parents traveled a lot," Elizabeth said. "How're they doing?"

So it seemed tonight's fun was about a heart-to-heart. Like the time they stayed up all night on the high school bleachers, talking.

"They're in Europe. Still working all the time. When I was out west, they sold their house and bought a condo near the airport. We get together. When they're in town." Elizabeth knew his story, how his parents prioritized their career over him, leaving him alone with nannies until he was a teen. "I'm grateful to your family for adopting me. Jeff found me like a lost puppy and took me home."

"I'm sorry your parents didn't see you as their greatest achievement."

"Will you see your children as your greatest achievement?" The pointed questions seemed a bit harsh, but he wanted to know.

"I must seem selfish and driven like your parents with all my talk of master's degrees and Fortune 100 jobs, but it's my only goal. I've never wanted anything else. Dad and I started talking about my career when I was in eighth grade. I worked hard to get into MIT. I overcame sickness to graduate. Now the end of the journey, the master's degree..." She held up her fingers. "It's so close. I can see it, smell it, taste it."

"Too close to give up now." Ryder held her gaze for a moment. "I understand. I came along late in my parents' lives. Their identities were in their careers. They loved me in their way, but hauling a kid across Europe or through Asia was not their idea of a good time. Just count the cost of career over marriage and family, Elizabeth. They can't all win."

"No, I guess not." She regarded him for a moment. "What about your brother? Where was he in all of this?"

"He was fifteen years older," Ryder said. "I was three when he went to college. Nine when he got married and moved to North Carolina, where he was ensconced in his wife's family."

"You used to say you wanted nothing more than a family of your own."

"We talked about it a lot that night on the bleachers."

Ryder set down his pizza, then took a sip of his soda. "Jeff told you I saved his life, but really he saved mine."

"By inviting you into the family?"

"Yeah, it was Christmas, and my mom was stuck in London, and Dad in Taiwan or some place. Karl had gone skiing with his wife's family. He said I could join them, but it felt like one of those obligatory invitations. Then Jeff came along, asked what I was doing over the holidays and invited me to stay with them. The tradition was for all the cousins, except the babies, to sleep over Christmas Eve at your grandparents'."

"I mostly missed out on that tradition."

"I was all in. Being with the Dorsey clan felt more like family than my sister-in-law's."

"We do have a strong family vibe, don't we?" Elizabeth opened a package of wet wipes. The pizza was good and greasy.

"Yes, and that story made me sound like a sad sack if ever there was one. I'm bringing down the whole vibe. How did you like that pizza?"

"For what it's worth, Ryder"—Elizabeth leaned toward him—"the Dorsey family loves you like their own. You'll always have a place at Granny's table. And what's not to love about Angelo's? Best pizza in the state."

The server refilled their drinks and asked about dessert. Elizabeth said tiramisu in harmony with Ryder.

"One piece, two spoons."

The jukebox changed to Frank Sinatra singing "The Way You Look Tonight." Ryder slid out of the booth and offered his hand. "Can I have this dance?"

"I'm not a good dancer," she said, scooting out of the booth, suddenly shy, feeling awkward.

"That's okay. I am." Ryder led her to the small corner dance floor.

"Even with your bum knee?"

"I forget about my knee when you're around." Ryder slipped one hand around her waist and held her hand with the other. Slowly, they began to turn, inching closer and closer until she rested her chin on his broad, firm shoulder. Ryder rested his cheek against her hair. "Have I told you you look very pretty tonight?"

She shook her head, warming all over. She'd gotten a few compliments from guys in her life, but never ones that made her swoon. Yet this wasn't supposed to be a date. This was just two friends dining out, having fun.

When the song ended, he looked into her eyes, but she stepped out of his arms. "We should get back to the table. Our tiramisu has arrived."

It was an excuse, but it got her out of the Ryder swirl.

Three bites into a creamy, coffee-soaked ladyfinger, Elizabeth's pulse found its normal beat. Even if she wasn't so determined about her MBA, she was definitely determined about love. Another moment in his arms and he might have tried to kiss her, and she could *not* let that happen.

When the server brought the check, she said, "You two make a cute couple."

"Oh, we're just friends," Elizabeth said. A little too loud. A little too forceful.

Then she tried to grab the bill, but Ryder snatched it away.

"Consolation prize, remember?"

"Yes, but I'm covering the garlic rolls and drinks."

"Tell you what, you can buy next time." He dropped a

couple of bills on the table, then walked out with Elizabeth.

Next time? He wanted a next time. There could be no *next* time. Ryder Donovan threatened to be a huge distraction. But deep, deep down, she wanted a next time. And when Ryder gently held her arm on their way to her car, Elizabeth did not pull away.

He held open her car door, but didn't want her to leave. Things were starting to feel good between them. If Sinatra hadn't stopped singing, and the tiramisu hadn't arrived, he'd still be on the dance floor with Elizabeth in his arms.

Despite her uptight got-to-get-an-education personality, she was easy to be with and Ryder wondered if he saw a side of her she didn't know existed.

"Hey, can you spare thirty minutes?" He glanced at his watch. "I'll have you back here by eight thirty, eight forty-five."

"To where are you kidnapping me, Donovan?"

"You'll see."

Two minutes later, they were in his truck driving down River Road toward Wade Reed and the fire tower.

They were quiet on the way over with the radio playing softly in the background. When Buck Mathews's first big hit came on, they sang softly along.

What a lucky man I am/ I've seen love.

'Cause when you walked in the room/I saw
    nothing but
You, you, you, only you, you, you
My heart will never be the same.
I just had to know your name.
From that day on, I knew…I'd never be the
    same.

Off Wade Reed, Ryder cut down a dirt road and through the vanishing rays of the setting sun, his F250 cutting through dry, overgrown brush and branches. Buck's song gave way to Foy Vance's "Guiding Light," and the romantic melody sank into Ryder's bones.

If not for the bend in the road and the ravine that folded down to the river, he'd keep on driving toward eternity. As long as Elizabeth was by his side. These thoughts, these feelings came from the secret places in his heart, bypassing all reason.

"Is that the old fire tower?" She leaned forward to see out the windshield.

"The one I supposedly bought cherrywood to repair." Ryder parked and popped open his door. The melody of "Guiding Light" cut off, but all of Ryder's feels remained. When he opened Elizabeth's door, he sank into the scent of her presence.

"It's beautiful here," she whispered, standing beside him in the hushed, pure quiet of the WMA. "So reverently quiet."

"It's my church every weekday." He made his way to the steps, shining his flashlight over the rotten portions. "Careful," he said, reaching for her hand.

He showed her the best boards to grab on her way up,

then followed. At the top, the summer moon was just making its appearance in the twilight sky.

"It's so peaceful here." Elizabeth stepped to the left side of the tower.

"It's my sanctuary," Ryder said. "Nothing preaches more than God's own creation. I wish He'd make it rain."

She glanced back at him, causing his heart to kick up a beat or two. "I love that you've not let the past make you bitter."

"Who says I haven't?"

Her white, even smile defied the shadows. "Me. I see it in you."

"Keep telling me that, okay? I have moments where it's not easy. If I were a dad, my wife and kids would be my priority. Even if it cost me money or a promotion."

Ryder waited for her to say something about family, but instead she said, "Thanks for bringing me here."

"I want to show you something." He turned her to the opposite tower wall, or what remained of it, and aimed his phone's flashlight. "See this? MD loves BC."

"Look at all the carvings," she said, repeating the initials. Then, "Pops and Granny?" Elizabeth traced the letters and read the date underneath. "Five-eight-sixty... May 8, 1960. Look, here's another one. And another. ED hearts JM. Ethan and Julie. February 2, 2018."

"I think my grandparents are on here someplace," Ryder said.

"Ryder, you can't destroy these boards. It's Hearts Bend history. I'm not sentimental about much, but these are priceless. You could add your initials one day." She shifted away from him with that declaration. "You know, when you meet the right girl."

What if she's standing in front of me right now?

"If I'm living here. I suppose. Sure." Maybe he should shove off, go to Colorado, stop this free fall into love with a girl who had no romantic interest in him. Who was leaving town in a few weeks without looking back.

"So when are you going to start repairs?" Elizabeth inspected another set of initials, noting one from 1882. "I'd love to help."

"This week. I'm still on limited duty. I have all the supplies. Travis is still hot about expenses I didn't accrue, but I'm not waiting. You're right, this tower is part of Hearts Bend history. A testimony of love." He motioned to the carved boards. "If he's finding hot water to boil me in, what's another bucket?"

Elizabeth squeezed his arm. "That's the spirit."

He laughed. "I think I'll take the boards with initials, trim them up, varnish them, and tack them along the walls."

"Seriously, I want to help. Let me know."

"When are you not working?" He winked at her.

"Okay, wise guy, touché." When she swatted at him, he caught her arm and pulled her close. "I'll text you when I'm not..." She ran her hand up to his shoulders. "Um, you know, working."

If she said anything else, he missed it, because every-thing in him shouted *kiss her.* But she twisted free.

"Careful," he said just as her foot broke through one of the weak, crumbling boards. "Elizabeth." He grabbed her hands to keep her from falling back, then aided her onto her feet.

"That was dumb of me." She bent to inspect her leg

under the glow of his flashlight. A red scrape ran from her ankle to her knee, but no blood.

"This is on me. I should've warned you earlier." Ryder examined her calf. "The skin's not broken. But get some antiseptic on it just the same."

When he rose up, she was so close he could almost hear her heartbeat. Ryder stepped closer and slipped his arm around her waist as the moonlight haloed her dark hair.

"You're so beautiful," he said.

"So...so are you." She was breathless and supple, leaning against him.

One inch, and he could taste her kiss. But as he dropped his gaze to her sweet, parted lips, he went cold with the realization he wasn't kissing Elizabeth Dorsey tonight or any other night.

"Elizabeth, I, um—" He eased his hold on her.

"We should get going." She exited his arms again, carefully sidestepping the broken board.

"Yeah, I promised I'd have you back by eight thirty, eight forty-five at the latest."

Ryder helped her down the tower's ladder, shaking free of his desires, blaming the moonlight, the dumb songs on the radio, and the stand-up man values his dear departed grandpa had insisted on instilling.

As he drove her to Angelo's for her car, they talked about the initials carved in the old tower, how Granny and Pops won the senior three-legged race at the Scott's Fourth of July party, and if the good Lord would ever bring rain.

He waited while she started her vintage VW Bug and headed west toward home. He drove to his place, windows open, blowing the last of her perfume around the truck's cab.

Despite the fire Elizabeth Dorsey stirred in his bones, he could not—would not—steal what he suspected was her first kiss. She could give it if she wanted, but he'd not take it. While the night bourgeoned with the sights, sounds, and smells of a perfect evening, falling in love with Elizabeth Dorsey was nowhere near a reality. She had goals and dreams. Even more, she was the kind of girl who deserved her first kiss from the man she wanted to love the rest of her life.

— ♥ —

Inside Granny and Pops's, Elizabeth leaned against the front door. Ryder didn't kiss her. Why didn't he kiss her? Her heart had been pounding so hard she could barely breathe. But thank goodness he hadn't. Because the way he made her feel…She wasn't sure she would've stopped him.

She glanced at herself in the hall mirror. "You know darn well you cannot let him kiss you."

"Is that you, Beth?" Granny called from the family room.

"It's the boogeyman, Granny." Her voice wavered with bottled-up tears. No, she'd not cry. Women bound for Fortune 100 companies did not cry. Women carrying the kissing virus were bound for a life without romance. She'd have to buck up. "He's demanding chocolate cake for a ransom."

"Chocolate cake?" Granny appeared in the doorway

in her yoga pants and oversized UT T-shirt. At eighty-two, she looked youthful, at rest in her soul. Elizabeth felt restless, full of turmoil. "You're in luck. I have one slice left." She made a face as she moved toward Elizabeth. "What's wrong?"

"Nothing." Then, "Oh, Granny." She fell into her warm, soft embrace and wept.

8

———

S he'd overslept, forgetting to set her alarm the night before. Her room was filled with the thin light of morning and the fragrant smell of eggs, bacon, and coffee from the kitchen. Yet she wasn't hungry.

After crying in Granny's arms, never confessing what bothered her, then washing down chocolate cake with a glass of milk, she hauled herself upstairs for a warm shower and a dab of antiseptic on her leg. Why, oh why, did his "not kiss" upset her? She was glad he didn't. Honest. The last thing she needed in Hearts Bend, Tennessee, was for her heart to be bent.

She always knew the name of this town meant more than the place where the road curved around the Cumberland River in a heart shape.

When she came down dressed for work, Pops and Granny sat at the kitchen table with oversized smiles. Sure enough, Granny had told Pops about the tears.

"Sleep well?" Granny said.

92

"You don't have to pretend I wasn't a mess last night." She took a glass from the cupboard. "I was just overtired."

"Sure," Pops said with a nod. "I've seen your granny that overtired many a night." He winked at her. So, they were having some fun at her expense. It came with Dorsey territory.

Pouring a glass of milk, Elizabeth reached for a couple of slices of bacon, then started packing her lunch. "Any leftover salad, Granny?"

She'd been eating far too much, and she didn't have the money to buy a whole new wardrobe for school. Her slacks, skirts, and suits were expensive.

"Hey, Pops," she said, retrieving Sunday's leftover salad and roasted chicken from the fridge. "I found your and Granny's initials at the old fire tower."

"You went to the tower with Ryder?" He cocked one eyebrow. A Dorsey special talent.

"He's fixing it up." She pointed to her leg. "I fell through one of the boards."

"Couples have been carving their initials in those old boards when they got engaged for decades. Before Cheatham WMA was even established."

"Did he propose?" Granny got up to refill their coffee cups. "Matt, there's more bacon." She set a couple of slices on his plate. Pops never refused bacon.

"Propose? Who?" Elizabeth whipped around. "Ryder? *No.* He was just showing me the tower. He's going to save the boards for posterity."

"So all those tears last night were about posterity?" Pops this time. Gee whiz, folks in her family were way too intuitive.

"I'm going to work." She collected her lunch and handbag and headed for the door. "I'm working at Ella's tonight."

"Beth?" Pops called after her. "You know we're proud of you. Graduating from MIT with honors was no small feat. We're proud you got into Wharton." Those words stung a bit, but she didn't correct him. She *was* going to get into Wharton. "We just want you to consider the good opportunities in Hearts Bend. There's no place like HB, Beth. This town is special. Same with Ryder. Don't say no to a good man like him out of hand."

"Will told you about the CFO offer?" she said.

"He ran it by me. I'm still chairman of the board."

"Pops, I'm grateful. I agree, this town is special. It boasts a major clothing line—O'Shay's Shirts—a country music star, a pro football player, and good grief, a part-time prince and princess, but that doesn't mean this town is for me. Not now, anyway. There's a whole world out there to explore. When I was sick—" Her illness was starting to sound more like an excuse than a reason. "Never mind." With watery eyes, she peeked at Pops. "I want to make my own way in the world. Just like our ancestors who landed on this plot of land a hundred and sixty years ago."

"Well, there you go. Matt, we said we're proud, so now let's believe in her." Granny patted Elizabeth on the shoulder. "Maybe Pops and I will head to the diner for supper tonight."

"That sounds lovely." Elizabeth headed out, feeling more emotional than the conversation warranted. Maybe she should heed Granny's warnings and rest a bit more.

As her little Bug hummed toward Dorsey Furniture,

Elizabeth's thoughts returned to last night, the fire tower, and the heat on her skin when Ryder touched her.

Why didn't he kiss her? Was she not kissable? He said she was beautiful, but that didn't mean he wanted to kiss her, right? He was just being nice?

Stop! What did it matter? She could not allow any man to kiss her. She was infectious. Or potentially infectious. Full steam ahead on education and career, where she'd commanded her own destiny, devoid of the whims of any human heart. Or the temptation to taste Ryder's beautiful, full lips.

❤

He finished his coffee on the back porch with Fred and Ginger at his feet, watching the morning light dissipate among the trees and thinking of Elizabeth.

He'd been confident of his decision not to kiss her, until it'd hit him: Maybe she thought he didn't want to kiss her. So did he mosey over to the diner later and confess? Or just leave it?

Besides Elizabeth, his knee bothered him. Climbing the tower irritated it. He also rumbled in his gut over Travis. Call it experience. Call it a God whisper, but when he collected his keys and headed to his truck, he sensed this wasn't going to be a banner day.

"Good morning, Ryder," Cheryl said, her eyes almost naked without her heavy lashes. She smiled in a way that made him uncomfortable. "Travis wants to see you."

Of course he did. It was becoming their routine.

Ryder dropped his canvas bag onto his desk. Taking a deep breath, he limped into the boss's office.

"You wanted to see me?"

The large man stood. "We have to figure out how to solve this problem."

"Agreed." With a sigh, Ryder dropped into the nearest chair.

"Since our last discussion, you bought more lumber from Dorsey? Teak this time?" He tossed an invoice in front of him.

"Come on, Travis, you know I would not buy teak. For what?" Ryder reached for the printed paper. Sure enough, his name and electronic signature were on the bottom line. "Come to my house. Inspect it. You'll find no teak."

"Are you selling it?"

Just resign right now. Call Enzo and take the job. "How long have you known me?"

Travis shrugged. "Since you were a teen."

"Do you really think I would steal from the TWRA? From Cheatham? Did you hire me to blame this mess on me?"

"Beg pardon?" Travis bowed up, chest out, chin raised. "Are you accusing me? I hired you because I thought you were a stand-up man, but I don't know. People change."

"Not *that* much. Not me. I'm not ordering this stuff. I don't know anything about illegal loggers. Where's the order for pine? That's all I've purchased."

"Accounting believes you've fudged your records," Travis said.

"I have the receipts."

"Whatever it is you're doing, end it now, Donovan. I don't want to see you in trouble."

"Whatever I'm doing—" Ryder stood. "Too late. Seems I'm already in trouble." At the door, he said, "I'm going to the dam today to check on the fishing and boating. Also, when I was at the tower, I noticed we needed to clear dead branches and dried brush. One stray spark and we're on fire."

Travis grumbled about a fire ban, then mumbled, "Dismissed, Donovan."

At his desk, Ryder opened the accounting app just to see what was logged against his account. But it came up with an error. He closed it and launched it again. It crashed.

"Cheryl, can you access the accounting app?"

She popped her gum, double-clicked, and nodded. "Sure can."

Ryder tried again and was able to log in. He copied his records onto a thumb drive and tucked it into his backpack. He'd review his records at home. In the meantime, he had work to do.

By the end of the day, he'd checked the docks and run off a dozen fishermen for not having a license. He hated doing that, but if he bent the law for one, he'd have to bend it for all. And he liked following the law. It helped him make sense of the world.

At home, Fred and Ginger greeted him like he was better than a steak bone. He let them out to run, then filled their food bowls. He fixed himself a sandwich, turned on a bit of jazz, then plugged the thumb drive into his laptop to check his purchase records. They were several months behind but showed he'd only ordered pine for the fire tower. Nothing at all about money to or from loggers. Or cherrywood. Or teak.

He expected a sense of relief, but it never came. Because the higher-ups were looking at something very different.

In the fading summer light, he worked off some tension by trimming the hedges around the back of the house and nailing down a few loose boards of his shed. He tossed the ball for the dogs before heading inside for a long, hot shower.

How was he going to figure this out? Travis seemed content to accuse him. Last night with Elizabeth and all the warm, comforting yearnings seemed an eternity ago.

"You're crazy not to fall for him," Tina said, setting up a couple of large garden salads in the service window.

"Why do I have to fall for him? For anyone?" Elizabeth clicked through the order screen, then retrieved a couple of frosted glasses for milkshakes. It'd been a busy day at Dorsey, and she'd hoped for a slow night at the diner. But they were slammed.

But the cherry on top of her day was Tina garnishing her evening with advice about love.

"Because at the end of the day, no one ever said, 'I wish I'd spent more time at my desk.'"

Elizabeth dropped scoops of vanilla into the glasses from the carton in the lowboy. "You can do better than a cliché, Tina."

"Not when the cliché is true."

Okay, maybe no one said "I wish I'd spent more time at my desk" on their deathbed. But they probably did right out of college or grad school. Why was everyone so down on her chasing her dreams?

Still, the residue of last night—the pizza, the dance, the music, the sunset, the fire tower, falling through, and crying on Granny's shoulder—left her distracted.

At Dorsey, she messed up her accounting. Printed the wrong reports. Emailed the wrong people. She ate her lunch at her desk, admonishing herself to "Focus."

Which worked. She'd just about cleared the day's tasks when she came across another expensive purchase from the Tennessee Wildlife Resources Agency for one hundred board feet of teak.

Ryder's name was sprawled boldly on the bottom of the purchase order. She recognized his signature, made with a large R, from when he paid for the pizza.

She reached for the phone and called Grant Hansen again. "Would the WMA order teak?"

"Teak? No. Never."

Elizabeth filled the chilled glasses with chocolate syrup, then slipped the first one under the milkshake spindle.

Should she talk to Tina about this? She didn't want to sully Ryder's name without evidence. If he hadn't ordered the teak, why did the purchase order note it was for the fire tower refurbishment?

Grant assured her teak was good against weather and water for a boat, not a fire tower, then admitted he'd forgotten to check into the cherry purchase.

"It fell off my to-do list. I'll check into these orders. See who fulfilled them."

What was going on? Ryder *was* fixing up his house on the hill. But he didn't seem like the cheating kind. And didn't his parents have money? Could someone from Dorsey Furniture be involved?

Elizabeth finished the milkshakes and delivered them to the customers at the counter. "Enjoy."

Heading back to the kitchen, she felt confident of one thing. There was no way the man who looked in her eyes last night was a fraud.

9

Sunday morning, Ryder found Elizabeth sitting by herself in the back of the church sanctuary. He slipped into the chair beside her and hooked his cane over the seat in front of him.

He'd gone without it for a few days, but when he pulled the carved boards from the fire tower yesterday and carted them to his little work shed, the knee revolted.

"You came to church again."

Elizabeth grinned. "Granny *accidentally* woke me up."

"There's no turning down Granny D. So, are you working the diner this afternoon?"

"No, Tina insisted I have at least one day off a week from Ella's *and* Dorsey. Granny and Pops are meeting old friends after church in Ashland City, so the family is on their own for lunch." Elizabeth waved at an older couple. "They come in every Monday night for decaf coffee, pie, and ice cream. It's a tradition they started their first year of marriage. They said they struggled a bit to find their rhythm, but if they went to the diner, ordered coffee, pie, and ice cream, they could only talk about things that happened during the last week that were good and what they loved about each other."

"So that's why so many folks go to Ella's for pie and ice cream."

"It's a good reason. Plus her pies..." Elizabeth gave a chef's kiss. "So, what about this afternoon?"

"I've got the boards at my shop, the ones from the tower. I thought we could start sanding down the edges and clean them up some. When that's done, put on a polyurethane sealer."

She regarded him for a long moment before answering, and he wondered what was going on behind those blue eyes. "Sure, why not?" She pointed to his cane. "I thought you ditched that thing."

"My knee didn't like climbing the fire tower steps yesterday. I made a couple of trips carrying the pine boards up to get started on repairs."

"I'll do the carrying this afternoon."

The worship leader called the congregation to stand. Ryder hoisted himself up, leaning on his cane.

"You can sit, you know," she whispered.

"Give me a sec," he said, adjusting his weight from one leg to the other. "I'll be all right."

"You're as bad as me, wanting to do everything on your own."

The couple behind them issued a loud, "Shhhhh."

Ryder laughed softly with a glance at Elizabeth. "I've been kicked out of class, out of bars, out of cars, and out of offices, but never out of church."

"Then shhhhh."

Okay, so they laughed through the first song, but wasn't church supposed to be a joyful place? Joy of the Lord and all?

When they sat for the offering and announcements, it seemed, and maybe he was making it up, natural to be there with her. Like she was part of him. Like someone he'd been looking for his whole life.

♥

The summer sun winking through the trees along River Road led her straight to Ryder's place. Down a partially paved path to gravel and dirt, she pushed her little VW Bug up a hill, then into the clearing where his small place sat in a patch of green grass.

Tucking her keys in the old ashtray, she grabbed the work gloves—shoved on her by Granny—and followed the stone path to the deck.

While she looked forward to working on the boards from the fire tower, she questioned her decision to spend more time with Ryder. *Liking* him was way too easy. But when she thought about it, going to his shed might "shed" some light on the mystery of the purchase orders.

"Did you build this place?" she asked as she made her way toward the deck steps. "It's beautiful." The house looked like something out of a magazine, with the cedar and stone siding and a massive deck.

"It was a dilapidated hunting cabin when I found it. The owner sold it to me for a hundred bucks, happy to get out of paying taxes." He patted the stone siding. "We're pals, this place and me. It barely sheltered me when it rained, let snow drift across the hardwood, and when sunlight hit a glass on a table, it nearly burned down. But it's cleaned up well." He stepped onto the deck, pointing to the shed. "You ready?"

"After a tour of the inside. Unless your underwear and socks are all over the floor."

"I picked them up just for you."

She was greeted by two very friendly German shepherds, Fred and Ginger, whose nails clicked across the sanded and refinished hardwoods as they followed them through every room. The design was simple but light and bright, fitting a man's cabin in the woods.

"So you went to design school before forestry?"

Ryder reached into the fridge for two bottles of water. "You live around Cherry Donovan for eighteen years, you learn a thing or two about interior design. Even with all of her travels, she was always remodeling one room or the other." He passed a water to her. "Be warned, the shed looks nothing like this."

Elizabeth followed him out with a final glance through the kitchen to the living room, toward the main bedroom. Not one piece of teak or cherry board to be found.

The shed was the same. She pretended to take a tour while Ryder set up the carved pieces from the fire tower on his workbench, looking behind things and into containers. No sign of luxury lumber. She turned at the whir of a sander.

"You want to sand or clean up the boards with this brush? I think we can use it to make sure we can read all the initials."

"Hand me the brush. If I use the sander, we'll have

nothing left." She sat on the stool across from him and reached for the nearest board. Ryder suggested she gently clean it off with the wire brush first, knock off the mildew and debris, then check on the initials.

Ryder turned on the old radio and music filled the shed, and an apprehension Elizabeth didn't know she carried lifted.

As he sanded the edges, she cleaned the boards, inspecting all the carvings. "SL and AW '82." She used a small carving tool to accent the apostrophe. "Ryder, wow, here's one from 1900. Fritz and Golda." She looked up at him, surprised by her emotions. "We forget history didn't begin the day we were born. That people lived and loved decades, centuries before us."

"The fire tower was built in the 1870s, long before Cheatham WMA existed. A blaze almost wiped out Hearts Bend with its one street and two shops."

"Can I ask you something?" Elizabeth said. When Ryder looked around from where he sanded the edge of a board, his lopsided smile reminded her of a young 1950s movie star. "Why is the tower so important to you?"

He set down the sander and reached for his water bottle. "When I was a kid, mad at my parents for leaving *again*, I'd ride my bike up here. Made my nannies furious. I'd climb up, pretend to look out for fires or someone in distress, and in my own way, talk to God. The tower was my sanctuary. I noticed new initials every now and then, and I started looking at all of them, realizing love wasn't something given when it was convenient, but something people committed to for their whole lives." He shuffled through the boards until he found the one he wanted. "This one...JCH and SLF, 7/1958 'til death 7/2005.

That's when I knew not all initials were made by googly-eyed lovers recently engaged, but by people who'd gone the distance."

"And you want that to be you one day." In that moment, she saw straight through Ryder Donovan and fell a little bit in love.

"Sounds stupid, but I'm hopeful." He reached for the sander. "That I'll fool a girl into marrying me."

"She'd be the fool to say no." This was not going the way she'd planned.

They were silent for a moment. The good kind where she didn't feel the need to talk. Ryder held up the board he'd just sanded. "If you have any ideas how to arrange them in the tower, let me know." Then, "So, are you preparing for when Wharton accepts you?"

"Not yet. Don't want to jinx it, you know?" She tried to absorb his confidence, but she was beginning to wonder if her acceptance would ever come. "Ryder, do you ever fear some things are just not meant to be?"

"Yeah, I do," Ryder said. "Every day."

10

The next week, Elizabeth gathered her courage to call Wharton, to see if she could nudge along her acceptance. Didn't they know it was mid-July and a girl needed an answer? But administration assured her that wait-listed students would be informed of their status in time for the fall term.

So she occupied herself with work. She'd not say it out loud, but she enjoyed working at Dorsey Furniture, being around the family—despite her grousing—and getting to know all of the longtime, devoted Dorsey employees.

There wasn't a week that went by without a birthday or wedding anniversary celebration, or some employee milestone. The lunchroom was perpetually filled with cake and balloons.

This afternoon, Ethan popped into her office. "Are you counting the days until you go?" She didn't have to ask about where.

"Almost." Elizabeth fixed on a smile. "Trying to enjoy

the lull before the storm of classes, study groups, research papers, all-nighters." She was starting to hate this facade.

"We've been talking around here and decided to throw you a Good Luck at Wharton send-off." His goofy jig made her laugh. "We'll celebrate."

"I think Dorsey employees are addicted to cake." But she appreciated the gesture.

"Lots of cake. And balloons." He leaned close like he was telling a secret. "Maybe even a DJ."

"A DJ?" Elizabeth shuffled the papers on her desk. "Sounds like you'll be happy to get rid of me."

"What? No, we just want to…Really? Will offered you the job as CFO because we want you to stay. We just know you got to do what you got to do."

"Eh, I was kidding." She shuffled and stacked the same papers. "Does, um, Will still want me as CFO?"

She'd not talked to him since the offer for fear of leading him on, but it would be nice to hear more details.

"The job is yours if you want it, Beth," Ethan said. "Think about it."

She was beginning to feel she'd hamstrung herself by only applying to Wharton for her MBA. It's just she didn't want to go anywhere else. Jordie had tried to talk her into applying to Kellogg, but she was so sure Wharton was a lock.

Okay, backup plan. It was time. If Wharton didn't take her off the wait-list, she'd apply to Kellogg and other schools for next year. She'd considered Notre Dame, but who did she know in Indiana? Boston University had a good program, but that meant she'd be back home. And after being sick for two years, she was ready for adventure.

Besides, she wanted to forget the years she battled Epstein–Barr, thinking she'd recovered only to fade again.

As for figuring out her life, Pops and Granny thought faith played a big part. Dad and Mom trusted in reason and intellect. From what Elizabeth saw of her cousins like Will, Ethan, and Jeff, faith, intellect, and reason worked together.

Elizabeth grabbed her phone to text Ethan, bundling her faith with her intellect that Wharton would see reason and accept her into their fall program.

Elizabeth
Get a DJ who plays '80s music.

———— ♥ ————

Ryder tried to call Elizabeth all morning in between chores around the house, but her phone kept going to voicemail. Finally, he rang up Ella's Diner. Not to bother her at work, but maybe Tina could give her a message. He was putting in Saturday hours on the fire tower and wondered if she'd be free to help.

"I shooed her out of here after the lunch rush," Tina said. "She's looking rather tired these days." She spoke away from the phone. "D'Angelo, drop another basket of fries. It's chili-cheese fry day, and we're going through potatoes like crazy. I need to drop this special and throw business over to the Fry Hut."

"Thanks, Tina, good luck with chili-cheese fry day."

"Ryder, hey, don't give up on her." Tina's advice came with the sounds from the diner's back of house.

"She doesn't make it easy."

"Most good things don't come easy."

"Yeah, but she has her plans. And to be honest, I'm not sure about my future."

"Are any of us?" Tina said. "You have to answer one question, Ryder. Do you want a future with Elizabeth Dorsey?"

Yes. The confession settled in his heart with a surprising *ca-chunk*, and it was too late to say never mind. His whole being knew the truth.

He was falling in love with her. Maybe he'd always loved her. But love never went well for him. Beginning with his parents.

"One more thing, Tina. What did you mean when you said she looked tired?"

"You know she has Epstein–Barr? Or had, I guess. Though the virus never goes away. Her granny and I are joining forces to make sure she doesn't work too much, tire herself out, and reactivate the virus."

"Yeah, she mentioned something about it. Thanks, Tina."

Hanging up, he headed for the kitchen with Fred and Ginger following, looking up as if waiting for a summary.

He knew a little of the virus. A coworker in Colorado struggled with the same thing. "I can't do it, Fred, Ginger. Can't ask her to give up her dreams for me. Not when she overcame something like Epstein–Barr."

The dogs twisted their heads in sympathy. Ryder tossed over a couple of treats from the bag on the kitchen counter, then loaded his truck with the lumber and tools needed for the fire tower. Today he wanted to work on the stairs.

When the tower came into view, so did Elizabeth's vintage Beetle Bug. Ryder stepped out, calling her name, navigating the weathered and broken stairs, his banged-up knee buckling once.

Still in her Ella's T-shirt, she sat on the far side, on a set of solid boards, back against the wall.

"Hey…" he said, picking his way across the twelve-by-fifteen cab, massaging his knee as he sat down next to her. "You shouldn't be up here alone. Too dangerous."

"Why? You come up here alone," she said with a soft smile.

"Yes, but I'm a highly trained TWRA officer." His laugh drew out hers. "I'd just hate for you to get hurt with no one to help. Hey, I called the diner looking for you." Ryder sat back against the wall, the breeze dipping down from the trees, cooling July's afternoon heat. "I wanted to see if you could help me with the repairs. Tina said you looked tired, so she sent you home."

"Granny has her worried about me. But I'm fine. I'm getting plenty of sleep. I drink lots of water. I have a doctor and homeopathic specialist working to boost my immune system."

"I had the flu my junior year of high school," Ryder said, pulling up an old memory. "My parents were out of town, but Mom sent me a giant stuffed teddy bear because I loved the one I had as a kid. Man, that thing freaked me out. It had these wild, glowing green eyes. Don't mind saying it, I turned him toward the wall."

"My parents took turns coming home early to take care of me. Or they worked from home," she said. "But hey, let's share a happy memory. We're always talking about the bad things. And please don't say it's the freaky big teddy with glowing eyes."

"No, not the big teddy. A happy story, huh?" There were a few, but Elizabeth's challenge made him dig deep. He'd buried most of his memories under the hurts and disappointments.

"Come on, Ryder. Spill. I can feel the boards rotting beneath us."

"Okay, okay, how about…well…minibike." He blurted the word as an image flashed through his mind's eye. "Wow, I'd forgotten the minibike. So yeah, when I was ten, Dad surprised me one Christmas. It was snowing, but I rode that bike from dawn to dusk with Dad instructing and helping, then he got on his motorbike and we raced down the long driveway. Dad, my brother, and me. They let me win, and we had a blast. Mom brought us snacks and hot chocolate. I went to bed like I owned the world. Best Christmas ever." He picked at a vine growing through the cracked boards. "I thought everything would be different."

"But it wasn't?"

"No, not really. We went skiing the next year. No presents. Fun, but didn't feel like Christmas."

"But you have that really great memory. There's always one or two that stand out."

"What about you? Tell me a happy memory, Beth Dorsey."

"My childhood was very different from yours." She glanced at him. *Go on.* "My mom was the queen of Christmas. She decorated the whole house. Bought the biggest tree. Everything was so magical and beautiful. Looking back, I can see how worn out she was by New Year's Eve, but she never backed down. Jonathan and I always had great presents, but nothing too extravagant. I guess one memory that stands out was when Granny and Pop came for the holiday. We were so excited we couldn't stand it. We were around ten and eight. Mom was baking, so the whole house smelled like cinnamon and warm dough. Big snowflakes piled up in the yard and on the tree limbs. You know how the whole world feels peaceful when amber streetlights shine on fresh snow? Dad had the fireplace roaring and Christmas carols playing. It was literally a winter wonderland meeting 'all is calm, all is bright.' Dad and I played a game while Jonathan helped Mom. Then Pops and Granny showed up three hours early to surprise us. They told Dad they were on a different flight. I thought, 'Every day should be Christmas.'"

"Maybe it should. Maybe that's what Christmas is trying to tell us."

"You mean keep Christ in Christmas," she said. "Keep Him in all things."

"Yeah, I guess so. Tell you what, I'd love a little Christmas weather about now." Ryder wiped his brow. "It's roasting in this box. Even with all the holes."

"Thanks for telling me the minibike story." Elizabeth pressed her hand over his.

"Thanks for listening. And telling me about your Christmas." He turned his hand over so her palm fell into his. "Want to help me repair the stairs? My knee is still roaring. We'll work for as long as we can stand the heat."

"Lead the way."

Yet neither one moved. The sunlight through the leaves, the curt edges of the breeze, the feel of her hand in his...this was the happy memory he wanted to relish.

———— ♥ ————

It was well after dinner with low-sloping sunlight when Ryder said, "That's all the boards I brought. Good work, Dorsey."

"Good work, Donovan." She slapped him a high five, liking that he clung to her hand a second longer.

They'd rebuilt the second set of stairs—tread and riser—with the nosing to be done last. It took way longer, and was harder, than she thought, but she loved it —the scent of the wood in the heat, the sound of the saw and the drill, the presence of Ryder. And she loved making something old and defeated strong and new.

Would that happen for her? Would she ever stop seeing herself as the girl with a virus that could rear its ugly head again?

"Can I buy you dinner? Ella's? Fry Hut? Angelo's? It's the least I can do for all your free labor. I couldn't have done this much without you."

She hesitated, removing the oversized gloves she'd borrowed from him. Spending more time with him meant feeling more. But hey, she was an adult woman capable of controlling her feelings. What's wrong with being around a man who made her feel wanted and pretty, appreciated?

"How about Angelo's again with a side of Pop's Yer Uncle ice cream?"

"You read my mind."

She helped him clean up and load his tools. But by the time she climbed behind the wheel of her Bug, she was exhausted. Her muscles and joints ached—not just from hauling and hammering. She had a headache, and maybe it was her imagination, but the lymph nodes in her neck felt swollen.

Reaching for her phone, she called Granny to let her know she was dining with Ryder. Then she dialed Mom.

"I think I need to come home," she said. "See Dr. Roth."

"I'll make an appointment," Mom said. "Does next week work? I'll book you a flight."

"Next week is—" Her voice broke with a whimper. "It's happening again. Just as I'm moving forward."

"We don't know that, Beth. Just keep your head up, be positive, and maybe stop working two jobs. It's okay to rest. You've made your point. If Wharton doesn't want you with your résumé, then they're not the school we believe them to be."

Mom, the corporate executive and Christmas queen, was also the consummate cheerleader. As well as a legendary secret keeper.

They chatted a few more minutes as she drove toward town and Angelo's. Pulling into the parking lot, she saw Ryder waiting for her.

"Mom," Elizabeth said, her voice low. "One more thing. How do you know you're falling in love?"

11

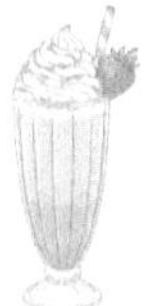

Wednesday afternoon, Elizabeth sat in Mom's beautiful white-marble and gold kitchen, eating a sandwich and downing a glass of milk. The last thirty-six hours had been a whirlwind—an evening flight out of Nashville and an early-morning visit with the doctor.

He'd just called to say the virus had not reactivated.

"I'm glad you came home, Beth," Mom said. She'd taken off a few days to be with her. "You can't afford to sit on symptoms hoping they'll go away. We saw what happened the last time."

"Wharton is a huge motivator."

Mom folded a dishtowel and hung it over the rack to dry. "And Ryder?" She grinned.

Right. The dumb question she'd asked Mom during a vulnerable moment. "Ryder? What about him?"

"Come on, he's the one who prompted you to ask about love, isn't he? You cut the call short when I started to ask for more information. Granny told me he'd moved back to town and you two have been hanging out."

"So? We had pizza, and I helped him work on an old fire tower. Hardly the romance divine." Elizabeth got up for another glass of milk. Why did she ever bring up love with Mom? "Granny sees what she wants."

"Come on, let me have fun with this," Mom said. "You didn't date in high school or college, and Ryder is an adorable boy."

"Man," Elizabeth corrected.

"I'm a mother. I can call him a boy."

Elizabeth focused on a long drink of milk. "You raised me to be independent. To get educated and go out into the world. Make a difference."

"I did. I want all that for you, but Beth, without love, your heart will never be satisfied. All the work will be meaningless."

Elizabeth regarded Mom for a moment. Growing up, she'd always been there to challenge and encourage her. Romance never entered the picture because she was too young or too focused. But now…

"The night I called you about coming home, we went for pizza after working on the fire tower, then took a long walk around town, eating ice cream from Pop's Yer Uncle."

"And?" Mom said.

"He's a good friend. I like him. We've known each other since ninth grade, but only during the summers."

"You always came home with a little crush on him." Mom wagged a finger at her. "You never said, but you talked about him enough. So I knew."

"Now you tell me." Elizabeth finished off her milk.

"He has a job offer in Colorado. His boss at Cheatham WMA is giving him a hard time about lumber expenses." Elizabeth paused. "In fact, Mom, I've seen some of his so-called invoices at work. His name is on cherry and teak purchase orders. But I can't see any evidence of it at his house."

"You've been to his house?"

Elizabeth made a face. "Yes, but only to collect the pine boards he's using on the fire tower."

"Did you ask him about it?" Mom opened the fridge for a Diet Coke, popped the top, and poured a glass.

"Should I? Or let him work it out with his boss?"

"Do you think he's doing something nefarious?"

"No, I don't. It's just not who he is, and besides…" She set her sandwich plate and milk glass in the dishwasher. "I don't want him to think I suspect him. That I'm not on his side. The other night…he shared some of his childhood with me. Parents always gone. Nannies coming and going. He had the flu in high school, and his mom sent him a giant teddy bear with weird, freaky eyes. He learned about family from the Dorseys."

"I'm sad for him, but isn't it a plus Granny and Pops were there for him? He already fits in with the family. You'd have a leg up on most couples at the start."

"Mom." Elizabeth snapped her fingers. "Wharton. Fortune 100. Don't lose sight of the prize, Vanessa Dorsey. Marriage can wait." If she married at all.

"Yes, but love…" Mom began. "When it shows up, you have to take a chance. Elizabeth, we work to make a life for love. Husband or wife, children, adorable pets, and crazy family vacations. The work is for you. Not you for the work."

"Can I at least get started on the work before you give me this lecture?" She roped her arms around her mother's shoulders. "Thank you for the work that gave us three dogs, two cats, one iguana, and a hamster that might still be hiding in the pantry. For the magical Christmases, the crazy vacations, our education. For sitting up with me when I was sick. For always telling me I could be whoever, whatever I wanted."

"I'm proud of you," Mom said. "Just don't ignore your heart in pursuit of your head."

They talked about Mom's job and her plans to redo the backyard landscaping until Dad came home. He asked about evening plans and how Elizabeth was feeling.

"The virus isn't active. But I am a bit tired." She retreated to her room to rest while her folks decided on dinner. Curled on her bed, she searched social media for any postings from Ryder. He never posted much but—

She sat up, smiling. He'd posted about the fire tower on Instagram.

@rangerryder: Fixing up this historic tower. Thanks @bethdorsey. Hurry back. Need my carpenter's assistant.

She rested against her pillows, still smiling. A post like this said *I like you.* But she already knew that, didn't she?

For a second, she was in his arms on Angelo's dance floor, swaying to Frank Sinatra. Ryder held her so close, stirring wild and wonderful feelings.

And now she was awake. Energized. And a bit scared.

Elizabeth hopped off the bed and headed downstairs, finding Mom in her office, reading emails.

"I can't fall in love. Ever."

Mom looked up, removing her glasses. "That's rather drastic. Never? Also, your dad went to pick up dinner. Barbecue. He'll be back in a few."

"Mom, I have a kissing disease, and I've never been kissed." Elizabeth paced around the office. "If I kiss anyone, they could get the virus. I can't do that to a man like Ryder."

Mom sat back with a sigh. "Then just be honest. Let him decide. And I'm still mad at your roommate for not telling you she was infectious."

"She didn't know. But I do. So how does it go? I just walk up to Ryder and tell him 'No kissing, buddy'? Or do I wait until he's almost about to kiss me, then tell him?" Elizabeth leaned over Mom's glass and steel desk. "I can't do it. I know how Epstein–Barr feels and—"

"Right, well..." Mom seemed to fish for a plausible argument. "Dr. Roth said most people already have some sort of mono or Epstein–Barr virus. They just never activate. And you're not infectious right now. You may never be again."

"But I could be. And Dad would tear your argument to shreds in court."

"So you're resigned to never falling in love?"

"Yes. Final answer. For the health and well-being of Ryder or whoever comes my way."

If God wanted her to fall in love, then He'd have to step up and make it happen. Heal her or something. And Elizabeth didn't have that kind of faith.

———— ♥ ————

This was a week of data collecting, doing surveys, interviewing fishermen about the fishing and resources and, in the quiet, wondering what had happened with Elizabeth last Saturday night when they'd dined at Angelo's again.

Ryder had dated enough to know when the vibe was right with someone, and he'd never experienced a vibe like the one he had with Elizabeth.

They talked so honestly. They danced in rhythm. They looked into each other's eyes. She rested her hand against his chest. He set his cheek on her dark, curly hair.

Then she jetted off to Boston, answering his text with emojis until Wednesday evening, when she said the doctor had cleared her for any active Epstein–Barr antibodies.

> **Elizabeth**
> He said I have to be careful. Staying in Boston until next week. Mom wants me tucked in bed by nine. Ha!

Since then, she'd gone radio silent. He didn't want to bother her, but man, if this didn't feel like his childhood all over again. Which wasn't fair to Elizabeth, but he was Ryder Donovan, after all, and people left him behind.

He knew better than to get attached to her. But she made him want to believe in every Buck Mathews love song.

Saturday morning, he rose early to work on the fire tower. So far, he'd avoided any more of Travis's tirades.

To be fair, the higher-ups were pressuring him to find the men cutting down valued and ancient trees. And to clean up his budget issues. Like the cherry and teak purchases.

Grabbing his tools from the back of his truck, Ryder cut the pine boards and started rebuilding the third set of stairs. He snapped a picture and texted it to Elizabeth.

Ryder
Wish you were here.

A car door slammed behind him, and Matt Dorsey headed his way. "Morning, Ryder."

"Pops Dorsey. What brings you out here?"

"I heard you needed some help. Woodworking is my specialty."

"Elizabeth?"

"She texted. Said your knee wasn't a hundred percent. Even an old man would be better than nothing."

"She said that?"

"Only between the lines." Pops laughed. "Give me your cuts, I'll carry them up."

The two of them worked in tandem—one cutting, one carrying—then rebuilding the frame where the wood had rotted.

When they took a water break, Pops said, "Elizabeth comes home tomorrow."

Ryder leaned against his truck. "I thought she was taking a few extra days."

"She's bored. And there's a lot of work at Dorsey. End-of-fiscal-year accounting." Pops finished his water and set the empty bottle in a bucket. "She won't be easy to catch, Ryder. Most stubborn of all my grandkids, and that's saying something. But she's worth it."

"You sound like Tina." Was he so easy to read? "We're just friends. And Elizabeth doesn't want to be caught."

"She's caught all right. She just doesn't know it."

"Who says *I* want to be caught?" Ryder ignored the low, grandfatherly "Yeah, right" from Pops. "Travis and I don't get along," he said after a minute. "A boss I do respect and admire has offered me a job back in Colorado. It's a good opportunity for me."

Pops simply nodded. "How about we take a break, grab some lunch. Ella's. My treat."

On his back deck, Ryder sat in his rocker, ice on his knee, the light of day evanescing. He sipped a cold can of soda and listened to the song in the breeze.

Pop Dorsey let the conversation about Elizabeth drop during lunch at Ella's. He asked a lot of questions about work as a wildlife officer and how things were going at his place. Was he still remodeling? Adding on? Then he regaled Ryder with stories from building his place with Granny D.

"Almost got divorced over it." He shook his head, laughing. "Once we got through that, we knew we could handle anything."

"So love isn't enough?" Ryder said.

"It's enough. The right kind. The kind that chooses love no matter the circumstance. No matter what the other person says or does."

Now, considering Pops's words, Ryder reached for his phone and texted his parents.

Ryder
Just saying hi. Hope you're well.

Mom responded right away.

Mom
We're good. Dad's in New York, and I'm in Austin, but we're coming home for August. I was going to text you, but I know you're busy. We want to see your place.

Ryder
Sounds good. I'll grill steaks.

Mom
See you soon. XO.

XO. Mom's version of "I love you."

Ryder
Love you, Mom.

Pops's talk had tweaked his heart a bit. Love chooses...

Fred nudged him for an ear scratch. Then Ginger. Ryder took a picture of the sunset through the trees. Then he stared at his phone, picturing Elizabeth with all her curls, bright eyes, and wide, even smile.

Dude, just call her. Pops D. was right. She'd be a hard one to catch. If he even wanted to catch her.

"What do you think, Fred? Ginger? Call her? Just to say hello? She's coming home tomorrow." Ginger raised her eyebrows. "I agree. Too desperate-looking, which I'm not. Sure, I can't stop thinking about her, but that doesn't mean I love her. Fred, what? Your tongue is hanging out. Are you saying I'm lying?" On cue, the large German shepherd barked. "Okay, what do I say? Can I pick you up from the airport? Pops didn't say she needed a ride. I'm sure he's got it. Oh, stop looking at me like that. I'll call her."

He dialed before he changed his mind. When she answered, he nearly hung up.

"Hey, Ryder," she said, rather loudly over the clink of glasses and cacophony of voices and laughter. "Just a second. Liam, move." Her laugh was buoyant. "I can't hear with all your big mouths." Ryder heard a male voice, shuffling, then quiet. "Sorry, it's so loud in the restaurant. I had to step outside. What's up?"

Yeah, what. Is. Up. Ryder? "I think I'm taking the job in Colorado." *Did you just lie to her?*

"What?"

"The job, in Colorado. I've been thinking and—"

"Really. Wow, okay." Her voice faded. "Are you all leaving? Okay, night, it was great to see you guys." Then back to Ryder. "Sorry, some of the gang had to go."

"Your Pops said you were coming home tomorrow."

"I am. A couple of my friends from MIT surprised me with dinner. They stuck with me during my illness. I miss them."

"Good friends are hard to find." Ryder pictured her, smiling, flushed with excitement. She was with her people. "Wharton won't be too far away for a weekend visit."

"I'll be too busy. Are you really going to Colorado?"

"It's a good opportunity. Good pay. Better advancement than here." He had to commit to the lie. He'd put it out there. He should've said *I was calling to see if you needed a ride from the airport,* but it sounded so lame in his head, so he dropped this whopper of a tale.

"I get it. Our careers are important to us."

"Absolutely. Hey, I'll let you go."

"Is that it? You just called about the job?"

"And to, well, see if you needed someone to pick you up from the airport."

"Will is picking me up."

"Then I'll see you when I see you. Glad you're okay too. No antibodies."

When he hung up he looked at Fred, then Ginger. "Not a word. Not one word."

♥

In the Dorsey family, one didn't need a reason to throw a party. So when Elizabeth came downstairs for work on Wednesday morning, Granny announced a Friday Night Guitar Pull.

"Will ran into Buck Mathews on a break from his tour." Granny handed Elizabeth her lunch, packed with grilled salmon, garden salad, and fruit. She made it her job to bolster Elizabeth's diet. She harped on her about getting enough sleep too. "They got to reminiscing about the old days when your Pops used to host guitar pulls and serve the best smoked ribs known to man. Next thing I know, Pops comes home with ten tons of meat, telling me we're throwing a party."

"With Buck Mathews? Playing in your backyard for free?"

Granny grinned. "Who do you think taught the boy to play?"

"Pops?" She grew up hearing about her grandparents' influence in this small southern town sitting in the shadow of Nashville, but apparently it stretched farther and wider than she knew.

"One and the same. Then Bill Hobbs took over with lessons, but Pops handed Buck his first guitar."

"That's exciting but I have to work at the diner, Granny. Tina covered for me when I went to Boston, and she has plans with her grandkids." Elizabeth reached for her bag and headed for the door. "Save me some ribs."

"I called Tina. You have the night off."

"Granny, you can't just call my boss and ask—" The look. Granny's *Are you talking back to me?* face, and nothing, *nothing* terrified her grandkids more. "Let me know what I can do to help."

Granny took her up on that offer. As soon as Elizabeth walked in the door Friday after work, she assigned her a few chores. After changing into shorts, a T-shirt, and sneakers, she started hauling things from the kitchen out to the back deck, where Pops had created a stage under a thousand lights swinging from the house, around the trees, and back again.

The scent from the smoker punched the air with the aroma of smoked meat, and the food table was already loaded with sides like potato salad, coleslaw, hushpuppies, salads, greens, cornbread that melted in your mouth, jams and jellies, chips, and fruit concoctions with Cool Whip and Jell-O.

"Granny outdid herself." Julie, Ethan's wife, set a hot casserole on the table, then turned to Elizabeth. "You've never been to a Dorsey guitar pull, have you?"

"First one."

"You're in for a treat. Some of the unknowns are better than the knowns. I saw Buck here when he was still a struggling songwriter." She made a funny face. "One of his songs made me fall in love with Ethan."

"Made you?" Elizabeth laughed. "Buck Mathews's songs cannot cast a spell over me."

"I don't know, he's got some powerful melodies. That being said, you ready for your first term at Wharton? When are you leaving?"

"First of August."

Julie leaned close. "Piece of advice? Study the course curriculum, clubs, the campus layout. Reach out to alumni. It'll help you feel more at home when you step foot on campus."

"I did a lot of that when I visited in the spring, but you're right, I should review."

From Pops's stage, players tuned their guitars. More and more folks arrived, filling the table with good eats. Elizabeth felt like she was standing in a scene from an old Hollywood movie.

Then someone grabbed her from behind. JoJo, Buck's wife, who Elizabeth's younger self had wanted to be like back in the day. They talked in the shade of the large elm, catching up, celebrating JoJo's pregnancy with twins, and making sure they had each other's phone numbers.

Tina arrived with her son Cole, his wife Haley, and their kids. "I left Lucy and D'Angelo in charge of Ella's," she said, holding on to her grandson with her right hand, her granddaughter with her left. "If the place burns down, I guess it's time to retire."

Pops banged on a giant pot from the deck. "Dinner's on. Let's thank the good Lord for the food and friends, then get this party started."

There was a lot of whooping and cheering as Pops started his prayer. Tina's grandson took hold of Elizabeth's right hand just as a warm, firm masculine hand slid into her left.

Ryder.

"I'm glad you're back," he said after Pops shouted "Amen!"

"Yeah, me too." Oddly enough, she meant it.

She'd not seen him all week, but he'd crossed her mind every day while reconciling accounts.

"About when you called that night," she said as they entered the long food line. "Are you really going to Colorado?"

"To be honest, no. Well, the offer is still on the table, but when I called, you sounded so happy, with your people, in your world, I wanted to seem like I had something going on too. How lame is that?"

"Not very." Elizabeth stepped forward as the food line moved.

"I didn't plan on saying it. It just came out. I realized you were off to grad school. That's where you belong. Suddenly, I needed to have something on the front burner too."

"Why do you need something on the front burner?"

He made a wry face. "Why do you think? I want to impress you."

"What makes you think I'm not already impressed?"

She looked back, willing him to see in her eyes how much she admired him.

"You're beautiful, Elizabeth Dorsey. Smart, ambitious, and all the things…I'm just a country boy with a degree in wildlife management."

At the food table, Elizabeth took up a plate and a napkin ring, grateful this personal conversation was covered by the dozens and dozens of conversations around them.

"Well, I'm just a city girl with a degree in management science."

"And the two shall never meet," Ryder said, reaching for his own plate and napkin roll.

Elizabeth glanced away. "No, I guess not."

12

As the sun made its way west, leaving long, warm shadows over the Dorseys' sweeping backyard, Ryder had just won his tenth game of cornhole, and no one else would challenge him.

On the stage, Buck sat in front of a microphone and started singing, not bothering to call for everyone's attention. Over on the plywood dance floor, lit with a string of round globes and solar tiki torches, couples began a slow sway as Buck's pure voice with a gravel texture sang over them.

Ryder looked around for Elizabeth, hoping to hold her on the dance floor, just as Buck changed the rhythm on the next song and the floor was crowded with line dancers.

To the delight of everyone, country legend Aubrey James joined the stage for a medley of old-time classics. After the initial explosion of cheers and applause for the Hall of Famer, couples started two-stepping around the floor and singing along.

Ryder faced the stage and saluted Buck. It was just like him to bring a big moment to his friends and family in Hearts Bend. Ryder was about to hunt for Elizabeth when Granny D. grabbed his hand.

"Come on, champ. Let's dance. Aubrey James is singing, and my two-step is getting rusty."

"I'm game if you're game."

"Hey, we're not too bad," Granny D. said, adding a twirl that moved them toward Pops, who danced with Elizabeth.

"Here you go, let's trade." Pops took Granny's hand and released Elizabeth's into Ryder's.

"They think they're so clever," she said.

"Your Pops came to the fire tower on Saturday. Gave me a hand with the steps, along with a bit of free advice. Said you'd be hard to catch." Ryder looked into her eyes as if to find some unspoken truth as they stepped around the floor in time with the music. Quick, quick, slow, slow. "But not impossible. I think he's trying to help me out."

"He's a fan of love."

"Exactly."

The medley ended, and with Elizabeth's hand still in his, Ryder headed for the dessert table.

"So, can I ask you something?" She picked up a small round plate and studied the slices of cake. "Did you order the pine for the fire tower from Dorsey?"

"Yeah, we always use the mill side of Dorsey," Ryder said. "Your grandpa set up a long-standing contract with the WMA that Dorsey still honors. Why?"

"Just wondering."

From the stage, Buck introduced an artist from Oklahoma, Summer Wilde.

"She wrote one of my favorite songs ever, and a country music classic," Buck said. "'The Preacher.' She's been hiding out in Tumbleweed, Oklahoma, raising a family and singing in the corner of a drug store. She's penned a few other hits, even one of mine, but tonight she's singing a couple of songs only Oklahomans know. Summer, get on over here."

The party guests applauded as the two embraced, and Summer, with long, wild grayish-blonde hair, sat in front of a mike.

"Thanks for inviting me, Buck, especially since I'm old enough to be your mama. But I love a good guitar pull, and love singing with my good friend Aubrey James. And hello, Hearts Bend, Tennessee." She began strumming her guitar. "I wrote this song for my husband Levi about thirty years ago. I still mean every word of it. Here's to Matt and Betty Dorsey and all you committed lovers out there."

As Summer began her subtle, romantic melody with Buck on the cajon and Aubrey singing harmony, Ryder set his and Elizabeth's desserts aside and took her in his arms, right there under the trees.

She rested her head against him, and he knew he could stay like this forever. Not only because she was gorgeous and curvy, bold and brave, but because she was on his side. He never felt confident that anyone was truly on his side. His parents, perhaps, but from a distance. Enzo, but he'd also been his boss.

Summer's rich, deep voice held out the closing note, and Elizabeth glanced up at him. He swept a lock of hair from her neck and searched her eyes for a yes before lowering his lips to hers.

"I-I should check on Granny." Elizabeth backed away. "See if she needs any help." She hurried off without looking back.

So, that was a no, then? It would take a lightning bolt to convince her he was worth the cost of her kiss and perhaps her dreams. Braving a peek at the twilight sky, Ryder sighed. There wasn't a cloud in sight.

He'd wanted to kiss her, and she'd almost let him.

"Beth, you all right?" Granny looked up as Elizabeth started collecting empty dishes from the food table. From the stage, Buck and some of the others were winding down the night by singing hymns with Aubrey and Summer.

"Of course." Her words caught as she stacked empty glass platters. "Wh-why wouldn't I?"

"I don't know, except you're collecting everyone's dishes but ours."

"Right." Elizabeth set the dishes down, then reached for a napkin to wipe deviled eggs off her hands. "What can I do to—"

"Come on, Beth." Will walked by, taking her by the arm. "I need a cornhole partner."

"Oh, okay." As much as she loved cornhole, she was a bit distracted by the arms and eyes and presence of Ryder Donovan.

"I see Will brought in a ringer," Pops said, standing at

the game with his partner, Grant Hanson from Dorsey. "Well, well."

"Blame yourself, Pops." Elizabeth picked up the square green bags. "You taught me." But to Will she whispered, "I've not played in a long time."

"You still throw the best flop of anyone here."

During her high school summers, the cousins cut her no slack as she learned, so she practiced. And got good. But it'd been a minute.

Will lined up on the opposite side of the board with Grant Hanson. Elizabeth stood next to Pops.

"I knew teaching you would come back to bite me. Watch out for her, Grant, she's *almost* mastered the flop."

"Almost?" Elizabeth grinned.

It was determined Pops would throw first. He bent slightly forward, jiggling his bag in his hand and, with a quick flick of his wrist, landed his famous slide shot, crowding the hole to prevent her from scoring.

"Got a question for you, Beth," he said as he threw his second bag.

"I know your head games." Speaking of which, Elizabeth had to push thoughts of Ryder out of hers. "They won't work on me."

"Why are you going? To graduate school?" He airmailed his third bag, landing in the hole.

She glanced at him with a spark of irritation. "Not going there, Pops." She winced as he almost holed his fourth bag with the flop shot. "Someone's been practicing."

Grant praised Pops while Will shouted strategy to Elizabeth. Stepping up, she was about to throw her first bag when Pops said, "I think you should take the Dorsey CFO job."

"I don't." But he'd rattled her. Her first toss, an air mail, missed and slid off the board.

"That's okay, Beth. You got this," Will said.

"Did you know I went to Harvard after Vietnam?"

Elizabeth peered at Pops, jiggling her second bag. "You what?"

"I went to Harvard," Pops said.

"Will, did you know Pops went to Harvard after Vietnam?" she asked.

"He mentioned it. Beth, less arm, more wrist when you throw."

Elizabeth's second air mail landed on the edge of the board. But at least she was on the board.

"I had no business being at Harvard," Pops said. "I didn't have any scholarly interest. I was just doing it because my pride wanted a Harvard diploma hanging on my wall. After all, I'd been in a war no one really wanted to fight. I survived. I was a man." Pops paused as Elizabeth tossed her third bag. A slide that just touched the rim of the hole. "But deep down, I knew I wanted to take over your great-grandpa's business here in Hearts Bend."

"So you quit?" Elizabeth held onto her final toss. "Where was Granny in all of this?"

"Pregnant with your Aunt Barbara, working to help pay the rent on our dinky apartment. Meanwhile, I was skipping classes and playing pool at a local joint. One evening, as I pretended to study, I looked out the window to see my pregnant wife slipping on the icy sidewalk as she walked home from work. She was carrying a sack of groceries. The food went everywhere. I ran down to help her, stopping dead in my tracks when I heard her crying."

Elizabeth made her final throw. Finally, her airmail toss landed in the hole. After tallying the score, Pops and Grant were up four points.

"How come I never heard this story before?" Elizabeth said as Grant began tossing.

Pops shrugged. "I tell it when it needs to be told. That night, as I lay in bed, pondering my life, I heard this loud voice in here." He patted his chest. "That I was proud. Too proud to admit Harvard wasn't for me. Too proud to tell your Granny the truth."

Grant's bag landed just short of the hole.

"Good tossing, Grant," Pops called.

"I'm not married, Pops. I have no children." She turned to her partner. "Will, do a flop shot and jump over Grant's bags."

"It's the principle of the thing," Pops said. "Will, nice flop shot. Grant, we've been hoodwinked."

"How is it the principle of the thing? Will, wow, you holed all four." Elizabeth collected her team's bags. "I appreciate everything you've said, Pops." Her first airmail shot landed in the hole. "But I'm not you."

Suddenly, a chorus of shouts cut through the night. "There's a fire at Cheatham."

Men and women scattered, hollering to one another. Granny stepped off the deck, dish towel in hand, her expression sober.

"Grant, Will, let's go." Pops dropped his cornhole bags and ran for the house. Elizabeth spotted Ryder running to his truck and caught up to him.

"Is there really a fire?"

"I don't know." He climbed inside the cab. "But I smell smoke."

Sirens began to fill the air. Party guests dissipated. From a clearing in Granny and Pops's front yard, Elizabeth could see small tendrils of smoke circling above the western trees.

"Fire," she whispered. And Ryder was heading straight for it.

13

Geared up, Ryder worked the fire line, cutting a firebreak as the blaze burned up a hill. A shovel dangled from one hand and a pickaxe from the other. He was exhausted.

"Ryder—" From the command center, Travis's voice came over the radio strapped to his side. "You watching the weather? A front's coming through. The wind is picking up."

"I'm watching it." After weeks of no rain, a storm seemed to be the answer. But a simple gust of wind could spark the hot spots over the firebreak. A crack of lightning could ignite the trees, which were nothing more than dry kindling.

The whole Wade Reed Road area was fire fodder. He'd seen a fire jump a firebreak once, but he'd also seen flames die out at an old, untended break as if it somehow knew thus far and no more.

Ryder scanned the area he and the others had just worked. Every officer in Cheatham WMA was called out, as well as the fire department and a crew of volunteers. He suspected the illegal loggers he'd spotted cutting down trees a few weeks ago were behind this, but the proof had become ashes.

He glanced down the line, checking to see if the wind would kick this thing up. Acrid smoke filled his nostrils, his eyes, his throat.

The Dorsey guitar pull, dancing with Elizabeth, listening to Buck, Aubrey, and the Oklahoma woman sing sweet hymns, was a world away. Moving on, Ryder continued along the top of the line, picking at hot spots, ignoring the ache in his back, arms, and healing knee.

His crew moved slowly ahead of him, but the wind, a force he normally loved, moved along with them. Ryder peered at his watch. Three a.m. More than six hours had passed since the initial alarm, and the fire still had life.

Pausing for a gulp from his water can, he studied the night sky. The moon and stars watching them at the Dorseys' were now obscured by clouds, and an eerie feeling slipped through the air.

"Rick, Chet," he called on the radio. "Pyle and Thompson. Let's make this our final sweep for hot spots. I have a feeling this thing is about to shift on us."

But he was too late. As they moved along the top of the ridge, they walked straight into a stand of spruce pines ablaze in a golden-orange crown fire.

♥

"Crown fire!"

Elizabeth looked up from where she worked alongside Tina and the other volunteers manning the makeshift command post, serving sandwiches and water to tired firefighters and volunteers.

She'd been at Granny's, stuck in a fret of "stay" or "go" when Tina called. "I need you. Meet me at the diner. We're hauling water and supplies to the fire command post."

Yes. Gladly. Thank you. She needed something to do. All she could picture was Pops, Will, Jeff, Ethan, and Julie, all volunteers, rushing off to fight a wildfire.

And Ryder. He would be in the thick of it.

"Crown fire?" Elizabeth offered bottles of water to firefighters coming from the edge of the forest. "Tina, what's a crown fire?"

"Where the fire jumps from the treetops instead of running along the ground," she said, inspecting the hands of a volunteer firefighter. When he'd peeled off his gloves, the backs of his hands were slightly burnt. Tina wrung out one of the cloths she kept in a tub of cool water and gently set it over the bright red spots. "Get some running water on it, Shem. Not cold but cool."

"Tina." Elizabeth turned the woman to face her. "Burning treetops fall to the ground."

"Yep, and on whoever stands beneath."

Then Ryder *must* get out of there. Glancing back to the hectic command center, Elizabeth inched toward the man everyone was calling Captain, hoping, willing to hear an update on Ryder.

"Get the helitanker up. But find our men first." The captain sounded frantic. "Donovan? Come in, Donovan."

But Donovan didn't come in, and Elizabeth half wanted to yank the microphone from the man's hand

and scream for him to answer. She'd never been this terrified. And by the expressions on the grimy faces standing around, neither had they.

"If we dump a thousand gallons of water on the fire line and they're up there..." The captain adjusted the radio volume as if that might be the problem. "Donovan! Where are you?"

Yes, Donovan, where are you?

Minutes seemed like hours. Tina called Elizabeth back to the water and first aid station, but she kept her ear tuned to the captain's radio conversation with the helitanker pilot.

"Any sign of them?"

"Negative," the pilot answered. "The scene is engulfed. The fire is going to jump to the next stand of trees if I don't drop water soon."

The helitanker circled an enormous spotlight over the burned-black region. The captain continued commanding Ryder and his crew to get out of there. They never responded.

Suddenly, the far end of the camp erupted with cheers as two teams working the east ridge walked out of the woods having won their battle. Among them Will, Ethan, Bobby, and Julie.

Thank God. Thank God.

Ryder, you best be okay, hear me? Elizabeth had heard stories of wildfires and their intense heat and fast-moving flames overtaking men, but Ryder knew how to escape. Didn't he? He'd fought wildfires before.

From behind, a strong hand gripped her shoulders. "How are you holding up?"

"Pops…" Elizabeth met his tender expression. "I'm not sure. This is intense. I'm scared for Ryder."

"The Lord knows what's going on." He drew her in for a hug. "I believe everything's going to be okay."

Elizabeth rested her head against him, desperate for him to be right, then prayed to the God of Pops and Granny.

The fire had encircled the ridge, trapping Ryder and his team of four. His weak knee nearly sent him to the ground more than once when his foot landed on uneven terrain. The fire glowed a couple hundred yards behind them as the flames rolled up the hill and burning coals fell from the blazing treetops.

They'd exhausted their water bladders—which were no match for a crown fire anyway. Nor were their picks and shovels. What he had to do now was get the men out of here.

He'd worked hotter wildfires in Colorado, but this one seemed to chase them. Still on the ridge, Ryder swept his flashlight over the terrain, seeking a way down to the creek. Through the howl of the blaze, he heard sounds of a chopper.

Command wouldn't wait much longer to drop the water. They had to get out. Now.

That's when he saw it: their narrow way of escape— an old firebreak. Hot coals were dying on its edges.

"This way," he shouted, shining his light on the path as he led his small company through the space, down the other side of the ridge, and toward the glorious sounds of the creek.

Hitting the stream, Ryder tugged off his headgear and splashed his face with the cool, clear water.

"I hear the helitanker," Rick said, scooping a handful of water to drink. "Let's keep moving, get out of the drop zone."

"Head east." Ryder reached for his radio as he started down the stream, kicking through burnt debris dropped by the wind. "Captain, come in. Donovan over."

"Donovan, where have you been?"

"In a ring of fire. But we made it to the creek. We're almost clear of the drop zone."

"Then I'll give the command to drop," Travis said. "Good work, Donovan."

"We owe you, man." Pyle clapped his hand on Ryder's shoulder. "You saved us. How'd you know the old firebreak was here? Or that it would work?"

"I didn't," Ryder said. "But I have a feeling Someone greater than I did."

———— ♥ ————

As twilight broke over the command post, shouts celebrated the death of the fire.

Weary volunteers headed to their trucks and cars, murmuring about the power of a thousand gallons of water hitting the burning trees. Pops left with Granny, who came up with bowls of fruit and grab-and-go snacks around four a.m. Tina had packed up an hour ago, out of food and out of energy. But Elizabeth couldn't leave. Not until she had eyes on Ryder Donovan.

Was he really out of the drop zone when the heli-tanker let loose? That was over two hours ago.

Blackened by smoke and exhausted, the WMA officers and local firefighters stood around talking, discussing the fight, assessing, taking reports, worried a hot spot might ignite again. But she knew. They were waiting for Ryder and his crew as well.

Yet the five of them had not emerged.

She stood off to the side, out of the way, whispering the only prayer she knew, "God, please."

Suddenly, a strong, moist wind whipped through the camp, and a sweet, drizzling rain began to fall. Rain. Much-needed rain. And five grimy figures walked from the trees and dim morning light into camp.

Ryder. Elizabeth ran toward him, pushing through the gathering crowd, and into his arms. "Thank God. Thank God."

Covered in smoke and soot, he only knew one thing amid the cheering and applause—Elizabeth.

"I was so terrified for you," she said, arms tight around his neck.

"I'm here now. All is well." Ryder gripped her tighter, his fears and weariness evaporating. When she stepped back, she swatted at him playfully.

"Don't ever do that to me again."

"Never," he said, roping his arm around her waist and

pulling her close again. "Maybe now's not the best time, but I love you, Elizabeth Dorsey."

"Oh, goodness, Ryder, wow, I—"

"I think you love me too. Only you have your plans and—" Fire always had a way of drawing the truth out of a man.

"Donovan." Travis tapped him on the shoulder, then shoved a bottle of water at him. "Need you over here."

"Rotten timing," he muttered as Elizabeth slipped away. But maybe it was for the best.

As Ryder gathered with the crew, half-heartedly listening to the debrief, hearing his name a few times, he was in another world. Never mind his throbbing knee, his burning eyes, or his aching body. Or all the speculation over how the fire started. Hikers? Campers? The illegal loggers?

He'd just exposed his heart to a woman who, in all likelihood, would never love him back.

14

Ryder woke late Saturday afternoon with Fred and Ginger peering at him from the foot of the bed.

"I know, I know," he said. "Who's the old dog now?" Laughing, he reached to scratch their ears. "The fire was pretty bad, guys. Ate up a lot of the Wade Reed area."

Careful of his back and knee, Ryder showered, then, in shorts and T-shirt, brewed a cup of coffee while he fed the dogs, then stepped onto the deck, gazing toward the burn.

His place was surrounded by green as if a fire hadn't ravaged a good section of the Cheatham WMA. As far as he knew, no park guests were caught in the blaze. No agents, firefighters, or volunteers had been lost.

He'd dreamed about the fire, leading his men into the thick of it and never escaping. He woke up every time, sweating and panicked.

Rick was a newlywed. Chet had kids in high school. He volunteered for the Rock Mill Hill football team. Pyle

148

and his wife had just had a baby. Thompson was his parents' only child.

At one point, he schlepped to the kitchen for a glass of water, the midafternoon sun filling the room with gold. He was safe. The men were safe. And Elizabeth's voice echoed in his head.

Thank God. Thank God.

Finding that old firebreak had been nothing short of a miracle. So yes, thank God. Thank God.

Back in bed, he fell into a sound sleep until the rich hues of the early evening flooded his room.

Thank God.

Ryder finished his coffee in his rocking chair, building a mental list of things to check, like the fire tower and how to write up his report. Yet really, all he wanted was a quiet night at home, a steak from his grill, a funny movie, and Elizabeth curled on the sofa next to him.

He wanted to smell the perfume of her hair and skin over the phantom scent of charred pine that lingered with him.

Setting aside his coffee cup, he tossed the ball for the dogs, and when they were panting and exercised, he headed back inside to scout the fridge and cupboards for something resembling breakfast. Nothing. He really needed to drop a couple hundred dollars at Cooper's.

His third—or was it fourth?—nanny had taught him to make a mean omelet, but it required eggs, which he didn't have. The idea of an omelet from Ella's Diner, with the best home fries ever and a side of pancakes, made his stomach rumble. But…

Ryder glanced at his watch. It was almost six. Good chance Elizabeth was working.

"Your old man made a fool of himself, y'all." Fred and Ginger listened with heads tilted, eyebrows twitching. "Told her I loved her. Yes sirree. Told her I loved…oh, but even worse. Told her she loved me too." Fred barked. "I know, rookie move. Never tell a girl how she feels. My nanny, Isobel—you didn't know her, but she told me to never tell a woman how she felt." Ryder pointed to Fred. "So listen up." At which time Ginger chimed in with a sharp bark. "Yeah, I knew you two understood every word."

Still, the question remained. Did he go to the diner for a late breakfast-dinner or opt for a premade soup and sandwich at Java Jane's?

By the end of his driveway, he knew the answer: Ella's. He had to see her. Undo the words from his weary, smoke-filled brain. He'd claim he didn't really know what he was saying. He'd apologize and be done with it.

He was about to turn toward River Road when it hit him. The fire tower sat right in the middle of last night's blaze. *Oh, be there. Please be there.* He headed left, finding the narrow road leading to the old tower, the landscape as he feared: charred, crumbling trees and burnt fields.

He broke through the rubble into a bowl filled with a July sunset to see the tower standing defiantly strong.

"No way." He jumped out of his truck and climbed the stairs, half expecting the remaining unrepaired steps to crumble, but they were intact. At the top, in the cab, he scanned the view before him.

Three hundred and sixty degrees of burnt woods, yet the fire tower stood. He could still smell the smoke and burnt embers. It would be spring and beyond before life would bloom again.

Yet the fire tower stood.

Ryder laughed, feeling a touch of the Divine. "I don't know how You did it or why, but...thank God," he said. "Thank God."

Now he *had* to go to the diner. Elizabeth would never believe it.

—— ♥ ——

"Everyone, a cheer for a hometown hero. He saved his men from the fire last night."

Elizabeth looked through the service window as Tina's voice sounded through the diner.

Ella's patrons erupted with shouts and applause.

"Lucy, on the house for Ryder the rest of the summer. What can I get you to start, Ryder? How about my Hungry Man Meatloaf platter?" Tina escorted him to her "premium" booth—the one she saved for special guests— in the front corner by the window. "Best seat in the house."

Ryder responded with something Elizabeth couldn't hear, but when Tina handed him a copy of the *Hearts Bend Tribune,* she guessed he didn't know he was the headline.

**Wildlife Officer Ryder Donovan Saves
the Lives of His Men**

She watched as he read, shifting in the booth, shaking

his head, handing the paper back to Tina, saying something that looked like, "I'm no hero."

Elizabeth set up an order of club sandwiches for table three, then turned to D'Angelo. "Can you watch the window for me? I'll be right back."

Ever since Ryder's declaration of love, she'd wrestled with what to say when she saw him again. Wrestled with her own feelings. Did she love him? In *that* way?

Now that he was here, she might as well face it head-on. After all, as a future Wharton graduate, she should be bold, strong, and able to finesse uncomfortable situations.

"Hey," she said, standing by his booth.

"Hey." He slid out of the booth to greet her. He glanced out the large front window, then at her, dead on. Brown eyes to blue eyes. "Look, about what I said at the command post…"

"It's okay." She waved off his apology. "You were jacked up from the fire, and your emotions were running high. I know you didn't mean it. So no harm, no foul."

"I didn't mean it?" The tone in his voice hardened. "I came here to apologize for telling you how you feel. For that, I *am* sorry. But don't tell me how I feel, Elizabeth. What if I *did* mean it?"

A passing patron patted Ryder on the shoulder. "Good work saving those boys."

"I didn't really save them. I just found a way…" He exhaled. "Thank you, Mr. Patricoff."

"I'm not trying to tell you how you feel," Elizabeth said, stepping closer, lowering her voice to keep this conversation between them. People were probably already texting Granny or Will or Julie something like

Elizabeth is talking to Ryder at Ella's. "I only meant you'd just survived a big fire and—"

"And I had smoke on the brain, sure, but I wasn't that out of it. I knew what I was saying." She stepped back as Ryder defended his position. "So I'm sorry I told you how you felt. About loving me. Also, I came to tell you the fire tower survived. I thought you'd want to know."

"The tower survived? Didn't that whole area burn?"

"Yep. Everywhere you look is burnt, except that old fire tower survived."

"Oh my goodness, that's…incredible."

"Or a miracle." She noticed his shoulders relaxing, but his voice remained stiff. "Sometimes things that should've died survive." He returned to his seat. "Glad we cleared things up, Elizabeth."

Wait a second. Nothing was cleared up. And he couldn't end the conversation with "I knew what I was saying" hanging between them.

He loved her? For real?

"Here you go, our hero." Tina set down a Hungry Man Meatloaf and large sweet tea as he tossed Elizabeth a final glance and reached for his ringing phone.

"Yes, sir…" he said, listening more than talking.

Elizabeth glanced toward the kitchen. She should relieve D'Angelo, but if she lost this moment to ask Ryder to expound on his comment, and thus settle her own confusion, she'd have to live with the swirl in her middle whenever he came around. Or bring up the subject again, and that was always awkward. Especially because she didn't want to encourage him.

"When?" Ryder said. "Um, yeah, I guess so, but not just me, right? The others too." He unwrapped his napkin roll and scooped a bite of buttery mashed potatoes. "Travis, we were just doing our job. It's why we get the big bucks. What? Are you serious? No, I didn't order that lumber."

When he hung up, Elizabeth sat in the booth. "Another rough conversation with the boss?"

"The mayor wants to honor us, especially me for getting my guys out."

"You don't seem happy about it." She pointed to the pile of peas on his plate. "You like peas? I hate peas. Mom used to serve them just to make me try food I didn't like."

"Peas are fine. Everything's fine." He sat back and looked her in the eye. "I'm not big on hero worship. Plus, Travis is still convinced I am buying expensive lumber for the fire tower but using it for my own house." He took a long drink of tea. "Is there any way Dorsey can see when the order was placed and from where?"

"I'll ask." She sighed as some of her inner turmoil faded. "Look, sorry I tried to tell you how you felt."

"It's okay," Ryder said. "I think we're getting our signals crossed. Just friends, right?" He took up his fork, focusing on a thick cut of meatloaf stuffed with onions and topped with a tangy tomato sauce.

"Oh, okay, well, glad we had our little chat."

On her way back to the kitchen, Elizabeth revisited the moment she saw him walking out of the woods, and nothing about it felt like "just friends." When he looked down at her, she yearned. *Yearned.* Like some soppy heroine in a novel.

"Thanks, D'Angelo," she said, taking over at the window, peeking out at Ryder. Nope, nothing about their relationship felt like "just friends." It felt like love.

"Did you hear about the celebration?" Pops said when Elizabeth came home from the diner late Saturday night.

"What are you still doing up?" She set her backpack on the floor and sank into an overstuffed club chair. Working two jobs tuckered her out.

"Reading. Waiting on you. How're you feeling? Long night, long day. Did you hear what I said about the celebration?"

"Ryder was in the diner when his boss called to tell him. Guess he's the star of the show."

"Is it true you ran into his arms when he came out of the fire?" Granny appeared from the kitchen with a plate of homemade buttered toast and a cup of hot tea for Elizabeth. She sat next to Pops with a sly grin.

"Is nothing sacred in this town?" Elizabeth sighed and took a bite of toast. "My friend survived a big blaze. What was I supposed to do? Shake his hand?"

"Have you thought any more about what I told you?" Pops said.

"No." Elizabeth buried any other replies with a sip of tea. "Why is everyone trying to redesign my life? I'm not interested in love right now. End of story."

"Your pride is tougher than I thought. I'm going to double my prayers."

"God is not interested in my love life, Pops." Elizabeth laughed and waved a piece of toast at him. "I'm heading up. Going for a long soak in a hot tub."

"Church in the morning," Pops called as she dashed upstairs. "I'll stop at Java Jane's on the way."

In her room, she closed the door with a looming sense of dread. She set her tea and plate of remaining toast on the desk. What was bothering her? Ryder? The way he backed off his confession? Was it Wharton? Lying to everyone about being wait-listed? Lying to herself about her feelings for Ryder?

Pulling out her phone, she checked her email. Nothing. Of course they'd not notify her on a weekend.

Sitting back, Elizabeth considered the shortsightedness of only applying to one grad school. She was tired from only five hours of sleep. If she wasn't careful, she'd get sick again. Yet everything felt off. She just had to get back to the mindset she had while fighting Epstein–Barr and regaining her health. Graduating from MIT and Wharton were her motivations. If she had a plan, her health issues didn't seem so in command.

Wharton may not have emailed, but her little brother Jonathan sent a quick note telling her tales of his summer antics as a camp counselor in Wisconsin. Elizabeth smiled through the stories, then hit reply, writing one short sentence.

"I think I'm falling in love with Ryder Donovan." Then she clicked delete and headed for that long soak in a hot tub.

15

"How's it feel to be the town hero?" Travis, aka Captain, settled in his wide desk chair, a dubious tone in his words.

"Uncomfortable, to be honest. And it wasn't just me but the whole crew."

"I'm giving you room on this refurbishment budget deal, but let me tell you, Ryder..." Travis angled forward and pointed his fat finger at the ranger. "I'll turn your hero reputation into that of a reprobate overnight if I figure out you've been pilfering the money."

Ryder tossed the USB drive onto Travis's desk. He'd gone over them again when he came home from Ella's. He didn't need Elizabeth or anyone else to find proof of his innocence. It was on the thumb drive. "My records."

Travis palmed the device and walked around the desk. "If I hand over your files, this turns into an official investigation."

"Bring it. I didn't steal or forge anything." He felt and sounded defensive but sensed the same presence he'd felt at the tower. *Humble up, dude.* "Travis, I appreciate the predicament this mess puts you in, but I can't confess to something I didn't do. The files are yours. If it becomes an official investigation, I'll cooperate."

Travis's hard exterior softened with surprise. "We'll get to the bottom of this, I'm sure. In the meantime, get with your crew, see what you discover about the fire. As for the commendation ceremony," Travis said, "false humility is as bad as pride."

Ryder absorbed the man's cloaked praise with a twist of wisdom and headed out.

If Wharton kept her on the wait-list, she'd get a different job that made her a better candidate for next year's application.

Elizabeth spent her lunch hour the next week touching base with recruiters and headhunters she'd talked with during her final semester at MIT, emailing some of her classmates, letting them know she was looking. She also circled back to the Fortune 500 company she'd interviewed with in Boston.

Taking a bite of her ham and turkey sandwich, she thought about school, which made her churn. She dismissed it as nervous energy. Otherwise, why would the idea of school feel like a drag?

"Beth, do you have the quarterly report?" Will asked from her doorway. "We're meeting with the board of directors in half an hour."

"I do except for a final number…Hold on." Elizabeth filled in the information, then hit print.

"We're going to miss you when you leave." Will paused at the door. "Ethan said everything runs smoother when you're around."

"You're just saying that so I'll stay." Nevertheless, the compliment boosted her sagging confidence.

"We're saying it because it's true," Will said. "And if it weren't, we'd be talking about your going-away party, telling you how you'll kill it at Wharton. You're smart, forward-thinking, dedicated, hard-working, and we love you, and we want to keep this a family business. But not every Dorsey works here. Like Raelynn and Marcus."

Raelynn was Aunt Barbara's daughter. Marcus was Uncle Steve's son.

"Yeah, well, okay." She looked away until a sheen of tears passed. "It means a lot, Will. Honest. I'll keep the offer in mind."

When he'd gone, Elizabeth hid in the private ladies' room for a short cry. Was this about leaving Dorsey and letting Will down? Or were her tears for her mounting confusion? Or for Ryder and everything she couldn't *possibly* feel for him?

Gathering herself and checking her makeup in the mirror, she returned to her office and was deep into the next year's projections when her phone rang. Ryder.

"Sorry to bother you, but did you get a chance to check those purchase orders?"

"No, sorry." Elizabeth clicked another program on her screen. "I've been working on the end of the fiscal year for Will."

"No worry," he said. "I gave Travis my files. If he turns

them over, it'll be an official investigation, but I just wondered—"

"Investigation? Are you okay with that, Ryder?"

"I have to be. Then maybe we can find the truth."

"Why would someone pin this on you? Why would Travis believe it?"

"He's getting heat from the higher-ups, so he has to be somewhat suspicious. As for why someone would pin it on me? I don't know. Maybe because I'm the new guy in town."

"Little Hearts Bend, Tennessee, has a dark side."

"Every town has a dark side."

"Every person has a dark side," Elizabeth replied.

"In my experience, that's very true. Maybe more people should listen to the preachers who talk about the Light of God."

Maybe. She'd be one of those people. "Are you all set for the celebration tomorrow night?"

"Will you be there?" he said with a hint of hope.

"I'm coming with the family. They want to stay for the Movie in the Park afterward. *The Lady Eve* with Barbara Stanwyck and Henry Fonda is playing. Granny loves the screwball comedies of the thirties and forties."

"They're showing old movies again? How'd I miss that news? Those were fun times when I was in high school."

"I remember watching *Grease* with you, Will, Ethan, and Bobby one summer."

"Now I'll have bits and pieces of those songs in my head the rest of the day." His laugh was soft and sincere. "So, I'll see you at the ceremony, and hey, thanks for any help on those POs."

"You should watch the movie with us," she blurted. *Do not encourage him.* "For old time's sake."

"I'll see. Maybe. For old time's sake."

Ending the call, Elizabeth hoped he'd *not* join them. If he did, everyone would be talking. And by everyone, she meant the whole town because she ran into his arms after the fire. People would think it meant something, and it didn't. Not much, anyway.

Well, who cares? Ryder knew where they stood, and that was the only thing that mattered.

Back to work, Elizabeth dove into accounts payable, which happened to be a collection of purchase orders and invoices surfaced from the WMA, all of them like the ones she'd seen before. Cuts of expensive wood, all bearing Ryder's name.

But he'd just called her. Told her he'd turned over his files to Travis. If he was hiding something, why would he give Travis the evidence? Unless he'd doctored his account, which didn't seem like Ryder Donovan at all.

Elizabeth clicked on the WMA's account and opened every purchase order and invoice for the last year, studying each one. Most seemed legit. All from a legit account. Most of the billing numbers had been in the system for years. When she examined the purchase orders from Ryder, they matched the fire tower invoicing, and the electronic signature looked like his. Ryder's *R*s were always the same.

The orders for the cherry and teak had different signatures. Like the person hadn't even tried. How had she missed this? How had Dorsey accounting missed this possible fraud? Elizabeth printed every PO and invoice, arranged them by date, and moved to the copier.

She called Grant to see if he knew who'd fulfilled the order. "No," he said. "The initial box is blank. Which shouldn't happen. You can't start the order without it being filled in."

"Do me a favor," she said. "Try it with two spaces. See if that saves the order."

After a few clicks, Grant said, "I'll be. Yep. Two spaces and the file can be saved."

"We've got a glitch in the system."

Then she called Ryder. When he didn't answer, she tried the Cheatham office and was told he'd left for the day.

Grabbing her bag and the evidence, Elizabeth set off to find him.

———— ♥ ————

A low growl emanated from Fred. Ryder glanced up from the computer where he was hovering over his refurbishment files, trying to see the numbers like an investigator.

He'd been so bold in Travis's office, but now? What if he missed something?

He raised his head when Ginger barked and hurried to the back door.

"Lie down, Ginger. No one is here." He clicked the printer icon above the spreadsheet. It'd be wise to have a hard copy of his spending...just in case someone doctored the files on the thumb drive. He was starting to be suspicious of everyone.

A soft knock on the back door stirred the dogs into a barking frenzy and proved Ginger was right.

"Simmer down, you two." Ryder peeked through the window to find Elizabeth under the deck light. He invited her in with "Everything okay?"

"I've discovered something." She plopped her big leather bag on the kitchen counter and pulled out a stack of papers, systematically spreading Dorsey invoices and WMA purchase orders across the counter.

"Invoices and purchase orders?" Ryder scanned the pages. "You mean you didn't come here to tell me you realized you *do* like peas?"

"Please, I will never like peas." She shoved the first stack at him. "POs with your name on them."

He skimmed the pages. "Can't be. Two hundred board feet of cherry? An order of teak? For a fire tower?" He shuffled through more papers. "I see my name, but that's not my signature."

Elizabeth shoved over his order for pine. "That's how you make your electronic Rs." Their eyes met. "I remember from the summers I worked at Ella's. You always paid with a debit card. And from Angelo's. When you paid for the pizza."

"Yeah, I never seemed to have any cash on hand." Ryder's gaze lingered on her face for a moment. "So where did these come from?"

"I think someone is charging expensive materials to the WMA and signing your name."

"Who's my enemy?" Ryder examined one of the forged orders. "Have these been paid by our finance office?"

"Yes, but something feels off. And the order was

fulfilled by someone at Dorsey, but we don't know who. He or she got around a glitch in our system. Which could mean someone inside Dorsey is part of the fraud."

"Did you tell Will?"

"No, I came to you first," she said. "You should go to your boss. I'll let Will and Dan Harper know."

"Elizabeth, thank you. This means a lot." Ryder stacked the printouts on his desk, then motioned to the fridge. "Can I get you something to drink? Water? Soda? Milk?" Now that she was here, he didn't want her to go. He peeked inside the all-but-empty fridge. "I can make iced tea or—"

"No, thanks. I appreciate—Ryder, I can't let you kiss me."

He looked up. What did she say?

"Th-that's why I avoid you when it looks like you might…I mean, maybe you don't want to kiss me and I'm making a fool of myself right now."

"I want to kiss you. In the worst way. But I get it, Elizabeth. You didn't want your first kiss to be with a man you didn't love." He stepped toward her, letting the fridge door close. "Would it be your first kiss?"

"No, no, that's not the reason. And well, yes, kissing you would be my first—" She slung her bag over her shoulder. "You said you loved me and…The point is, I can never kiss a man, ever. On the lips, anyway. I could pass on the Epstein–Barr virus, which is the big brother of mono. I can't do that to you or anyone."

"I see," he said. "But you're not infectious?"

"Not now, no. But the virus can flare up and—"

"What if I didn't care about a possible virus?" He came around the kitchen island to where she stood in the living room. "What if I thought you were worth the risk?"

"I'd say you should care." She glanced down at Ginger, who was sprawled at her feet. "I wanted to be honest. With you. With myself. This is why grad school and a career are more important to me than ever. Love may not be in the cards for me. I don't want to pass this virus on to anyone I love. I'd feel like a bad princess in a Grimms' fairy tale."

She was so serious. As if a virus truly rendered her loveless. "Elizabeth, I'm pretty sure people who've had mono or Epstein–Barr marry and live full, romantic lives."

"Maybe, but that's not a risk I'm willing to take."

"Even for love?"

"Even for love."

"Elizabeth, it doesn't matter to me. Are you sure this is not just an excuse to—"

"If you want me to go with you to your boss, let me know." She bent to scratch Ginger behind the ears.

"Yeah, okay, if you don't mind. That'd be great."

"Text me when," she said, walking around him for the kitchen door.

Ryder startled a little as the door softly clicked closed behind her.

16

Going to see Ryder made her late for a shift at Ella's. But she'd texted Tina she'd be in as soon as possible.

She also felt a bit silly bringing up the kiss with Ryder, all in the name of honesty. Replaying the conversation in her head on her way home, she concluded she sounded more rude than honest. Also, a bit of a martyr.

...I can never kiss a man, ever.

Should she apologize? Do a take-back on the whole conversation? Maybe she would kiss a man, one day, if they pledged themselves in a lifelong commitment. But not during a summer romance. Ugh, relationships...This was why she preferred school and career, logic and order. On the job, she knew the rules. Knew the boundaries.

Granny caught her when she walked into the kitchen from the mud room. "Good, you're home for dinner." She was removing a roasted chicken from the oven. "Set a place at the table."

"Actually, I'm late for Ella's. Tina needs help. One of the servers called in sick," Elizabeth tried to pinch a piece from the chicken, but the steaming bird was too hot. "I took some papers over to Ryder."

"What sort of papers?" Granny said without looking up. She was pouring the juices into her gravy mixture. "And you can tell Tina no. What happened to our pact to keep you from working so much?"

"I'm fine, Granny. I promise." Though she was feeling tired today. "Papers. Purchase orders and invoices." She paused on her way to the stairs. "Granny, how did you know you loved Pops?"

Granny whisked the gravy while she thought. "I had a list. Your Pops ticked off all but two, and it turned out to be a good thing. He was handsome, kind, generous, loved Jesus, and worked hard. He treated his mother well. Always look at how the one you love treats his parents. If they are rude and unforgiving, that will spill over into your relationship."

"What if his parents weren't around much?"

Granny eyed her. "Ryder?"

"Just asking, Granny."

"You see how Ryder treats Pops and me. When his parents are in town, I know for a fact he goes out of his way to spend time with them."

Elizabeth came back to the stove. She needed Granny's wisdom to wrangle with her thoughts. "We've almost kissed a few times."

"I see." Granny never broke rhythm on whisking her gravy.

"I told him tonight that I couldn't kiss him because of EBV. I think I sounded kind of cold." Elizabeth picked at the small thread protruding from the side of Granny's apron. "I should apologize." She gave Granny a forced smile, waiting for her approval.

"Darling." Granny took her by the shoulders. "It's okay to not kiss a man. It's okay to be honest about why. But is your dormant virus really the reason? Or are you Pops's mini-me, determined to do your will above all else?" Back to the bubbling gravy. Whisk, whisk, whisk. "I don't think you can pass on the virus if you're not infectious. Did you ask your doctor?"

Elizabeth sighed. "So much to unpack here, Granny. First of all, I'm only like Pops in that I know what I want. Second, I know I'm not infectious, but shouldn't I at least present Ryder or whoever with a doctor's note?"

Granny's laugh filled the kitchen. "Well, you didn't get your romantic inclinations from me or Pops." She clicked off the stove and set the gravy aside. "Let me ask you something. Have you ever really given love and Hearts Bend a chance? Does a Fortune 100 career mean that much to you? If so, why did you spend your summers here, with your Pops and me and the family, when you were a teen? Why didn't you intern at one of those big Boston companies? I know for a fact your dad secured a place for you at his firm."

"I wanted a career, yes. I just didn't want to start at sixteen."

"Fair enough, but one final question. Are you sure your ambition isn't just in your head but not in your heart?"

Granny had a way of drilling down. Her question sat on Elizabeth as she changed into her Ella's uniform. As she drove down First Avenue in her restored VW Bug. As she shot Tina a quick "Sorry I'm late" and stepped up to command the service window.

She was starting to sound like a broken record. Grad school, grad school, career, career. It's not that she wasn't open to other ideas, it's just she'd lost so much time being sick. And to be honest, she didn't have any other ideas. She hated to not finish what she'd started.

Yet if any man could make her want to risk it all, it was Ryder Donovan. Sigh. Too many questions. Too, too many.

Ella's was hopping for the dinner rush. Another server called off, so Tina was busy filling in where she could, but she loved being out on the floor with the customers.

The restaurant was often a destination for out-of-towners. Nashville had Pancake Pantry. Hearts Bend had Ella's Diner.

Around eight thirty, the rush had faded. Elizabeth started cleaning up while Tina ran numbers from the POS machine.

"Have you seen Ryder lately?" she said rather casually.

"Today," Elizabeth said. "I had to take some things to him from the Dorsey Mill side of Dorsey Furniture."

"And?"

"And what?" Elizabeth dumped out the lettuce fragments from the salad station, then asked one of the busboys to get a bag from the walk-in refrigerator. "I gave him the stuff."

Tina laughed. "Okay…I won't ask what *stuff*. How's he doing? After the fire?"

"Well enough."

"You're never going to admit it, are you?" Tina leaned against the counter, her arms folded. "He's a good man."

"You want me to admit Ryder is a good man? Easy. He is."

"No, I want you to admit you two would be great together."

"That's not what you said."

"No, I want you to say it."

Elizabeth notified one of the servers his order was up. "Okay, maybe I will say it. After you go out with Marty."

Tina exhaled, made a face, and headed for her office.

"Two can play this game," Elizabeth called after her.

Tina's input layered up with Granny's. Could she love Hearts Bend? Would she and Ryder be a good couple? What about his job offer in Colorado? They were bound for different roads. At least for now.

Grabbing a glass, Elizabeth walked out to the soda machine. Sometimes the fizz of an icy cold soda was the only way to slake a thirst. She was about to head back to the kitchen when she saw Ryder in a booth by the window. He smiled sheepishly, giving her the two-finger wave.

She slipped in the seat across from him. "The special is good. Tina's spaghetti and meatballs with garlic bread and side salad. She doesn't make it very often. It competes too much with Angelo's, she says."

"Then I'll have the special." Ryder closed his menu and shoved it to the end of the table. "Elizabeth—"

"About what I said earlier...I must've sounded like an idiot. My attempt at being honest came off as rude."

"You weren't rude." He had a way with his smile that

made everything he said feel true. "It's good to know if you're not kissing me, you're not kissing any other man."

"Well, that's one way of looking at it." Could she do this? Sit at a table across from Ryder Donovan the rest of her life? Could she kiss him without thinking of the virus?

Could she get married, buy a house, and maybe paint it blue? Could she have children, drive a van, then sit in a lawn chair with all the other parents watching their children run up and down the soccer or football field? She'd never really thought about any of it before, and suddenly she could think of nothing else.

"I never thought I'd get married, you know. Not in my twenties, anyway."

"I always thought I'd marry young. Being a lonely, almost-only child, I really wanted a family." He twisted the straw paper around his fingers. "I still do."

It seemed they were having a conversation about their relationship *without* *actually* having the conversation.

"Can you meet me at the WMA offices in the morning? Eight o'clock?" he said.

"I'll be there." Elizabeth slid from the booth with her soda. "Do you want dessert too? Remember Tina's edict. On the house for our smoke-brain heroes."

"Do you think I'm a hero?"

"Yes, I really do."

— ♥ —

"Cheryl, is Travis in?" Ryder paused at the admin's desk, covered with stickies, calendars, and manuals. Cheryl adhered to an eclectic organizational style.

"In his office." She was tweaking the return of her long, fake eyelashes with tweezers and a hand mirror.

"Am I hauling you into my controversy?" Ryder said to Elizabeth, flashing the collection of invoices and purchase orders he held in his hand.

"Consider me your backup in case he doesn't believe you."

Ryder knocked once, entering when Travis groused, "Enter." His boss looked at Elizabeth. "And who is this?"

"Elizabeth Dorsey, from Dorsey Furniture accounting." He plopped the evidence of his innocence on the desk. "She found these."

"These being…?" Travis grabbed for the stack of papers, then rocked back in his wide, leather chair.

"Purchases in my name, but not my signature, Travis. Someone is ordering teak and cherry from the mill arm of Dorsey and charging it to my fire tower account."

"We don't know who fulfilled the orders at Dorsey," Elizabeth added. "They abused a bug in the system."

With a grunt, Travis rocked forward and spread the copies across his desk. "You found these?" He looked at Elizabeth. "Maybe Ryder knows someone at Dorsey Mill."

"I've been to Ryder's workshop, his house, and the fire tower. There is not one board of cherry or teak. Pine, yes, but that's all."

"Maybe he's selling it. Making a profit. Maybe he's in cahoots with the men he caught cutting timber."

"You've got to be kidding me." Travis was a piece of work. A real piece of—

"If you believe that, why is he still here?" Elizabeth said. "Why haven't you fired him? Maybe you're the one ordering cherry and teak."

Travis fired out of his chair. "Excuse me, but I never—"

"Doesn't feel so good being unjustly accused, does it?" Elizabeth was unflinching.

Ryder grinned. He'd kiss her if he could. "Travis, someone is ordering lumber and charging it to us. To my fire tower account. You should report this."

Travis picked through the evidence again, a shadow falling over his face. "All right, Donovan. For now, it looks like you've cleared your name. But the agency will still have to investigate."

"I understand. And thank you, sir." Ryder extended his hand to Travis.

It took a second, but the older man grasped his hand in a firm shake. "I'll take it from here. You keep working on that old Hearts Bend fire tower."

They were outside by Elizabeth's car before either one spoke. "I feel like I've lost a thousand pounds," Ryder said, leaning against her car. "Thank you."

She stared toward the brick office. "He accused you and made no apology? No, thank you for having integrity. Being honest."

"He will. Eventually."

Elizabeth squeezed his arm. "I'm in your corner, you know."

"Feels good to be defended." Ryder took hold of her arm. "Even though my folks weren't around much when

I was a kid, they always defended me." He grinned and slid his hand down to hers. "If I deserved it."

"Ryder, do you forgive them for not being around?"

"I have my days, but yeah, I do. What's the alternative? Living mad? Making myself a victim? No thanks."

His admission tugged more on her heart than his *I love you*. "When will you work on the fire tower again?" She pulled the VW keys from her handbag.

"Saturday. Want to help? You should see it, Beth. It looks so regal yet lonely, sitting among the burnt area."

"Is that common? For something to be left behind after a fire?"

"Not common at all. But that fire tower represents all the good about Hearts Bend. Folks helping folks. Being a close-knit community. Hiding in the shadows of Nashville. Maybe even hiding in the shadow of God."

Friday night, the Kids Theater was lit with lights and excited buzz as locals cheered their heroes —the firefighters and WMA officers who stopped the fire.

As the ceremony ended, Elizabeth exited a row of Dorseys with Granny and Pops. On stage, the heroes were taking pictures, holding up their commendations. Ryder stood in the center of it all, smiling, shaking hands.

That's when an odd sensation flipped through her. Like she was proud of him. As if he was hers. When the mayor singled him out during his speech for leading his team to safety during the crown fire, she felt as if she might burst with pride. For him. Not herself.

"He's a good man," Will said, coming up behind her as she entered the theater's lobby.

"All of them are good men."

"But not all of them are special to you."

Saying nothing, she pushed through the doors and into the summer's evening sun as it draped gold flags between the buildings and through the streets. Gardenia Park was circled with food trucks, and a brass band played patriotic songs to continue the celebration. Will followed her onto the sidewalk, gathering with the rest of the Dorseys.

"Hey, Will, did you have a chance to read my email?" she said.

"Yeah, took a peek right before I left work."

"You need a new accounting system." For the past two days, Elizabeth had been looking into the WMA fraud, finding more anomalies along the way. Besides the bug in order fulfillment, she'd found other glitches and back doors in the antique system. It was possible for Dorsey employees to hide fraud or skim a few dollars into a private account. Which, so far, she'd found no evidence of.

"We've duct-taped our old one together for so long," Will said. "All our processes work. Everyone knows their job."

"You may be losing money, Will. Someone inside Dorsey cut that lumber. We don't know who. And someone picked it up."

"Dan said the same thing. He's noticed accounts marked 'paid,' but when he reconciled, the dollars didn't add up. He's personally checking all log-ons and accounts." He sighed. "I won't say how much we'd love for you to stay on board. Help bring us all the way into the twenty-first century."

"That's good," she said. "Since you already said it." And now would be a good time to tell him about her recent decision.

"I need a few days off next week to go up to Wharton.

I need to…" What? Try to get in? "Check on my courses and find a place to live."

"If you need to go, go." Will roped her in for a side hug. He was probably her favorite cousin, but his kindness was making it harder and harder to leave. "I'm going to miss you, by the way," he said. "Are you taking it easy? Granny said you're still pulling a heavy load at Ella's."

"Not a heavy load. A few nights a week and part of Saturdays."

He gave her the big-cousin eye, then greeted some friends. Elizabeth hung back, waiting for Ryder to exit. Catching his eye, she smiled and waved. He headed her way but was cut off by a group of congratulators.

Elizabeth moved on, finding Granny, offering to buy her a hot dog from the Fry Hut's truck. She'd just lathered onions and mustard on her hot dog when Ryder came up behind her.

"Care to get out of here?"

Elizabeth set down the mustard bottle. "Lead the way."

⸻ ♥ ⸻

They sat on the steps of the fire tower, surveying the burnt region and how the sunset trimmed the black horizon with gold.

"It's so stark yet so beautiful," Elizabeth said. "Is it wrong to say that?"

"No. Fires are damaging and horrendous, yet the regrowth can be so powerful."

As he spoke, a gentle summer rain began to fall from the singular cloud passing over them.

Ryder glanced at Elizabeth, ready to make a run for it, but she didn't move except to lift her face to the rain, eyes closed, the napkin from her hot dog wadded in her hand.

"Pops would say God was refreshing us and the land," she said quietly.

Ryder almost felt like an eavesdropper on a private conversation. Yet a peace that only comes with the rain of heaven settled over him.

As the soft drops soaked in, his skin cooled, and his heart warmed with love for this woman. If he kissed her, he'd sink all the way in. So in many ways, having the kissing question off the table was a relief.

"Granny says I haven't given love or Hearts Bend a chance." She rested against the side of the tower, where a post held the rickety steps against the fire tower cabin. "That my ambition is in my head, but not my heart."

"Granny D. never struggled to speak her mind. All that matters is what you think. What you want."

"I know. I mean, I've been taught to consider all sides. To hear the other argument, learn what I don't know." She shifted her gaze to him. "I've decided to go to Wharton next week."

"You were accepted? Why didn't you tell me?"

"No, I'm still wait-listed." By her sigh and shift in her posture, she was weary of it all. "I'm going to see if I can't charm them into letting me in."

"What do your Granny and Pops say?"

"I've not told anyone but you. Too embarrassed. For all my big talk, I'm not even in the fall class."

"Doesn't mean you won't get in. There's always next year." He shifted a little closer to her, mopping up the water on the thirsty tower steps with his jeans.

"I don't want to wait another year."

"Is there any truth to what your granny said?"

"I don't know." She looked away. "But I *have* to try."

If she was determined to go, let her go. Saying his heart thumped whenever she was around or that he still wanted to kiss her so badly his lips buzzed sounded desperate, like a badly penned poem.

"Enzo texted he still wants me in Colorado." He wasn't sure why he brought it up. Maybe so he didn't look like the "stuck" hometown guy next to her ambition.

Another cloud passed over them, and for a solid thirty seconds, the rain fell in buckets, soaking them to the bone. As suddenly as it appeared, the cloud drew up its shower curtain and slowly drifted toward the horizon, allowing the sunset to rim the evening with gold.

"I guess that cloud told us." Elizabeth swiped watery streaks of black mascara from her cheeks. When she turned to Ryder, they laughed in harmony. "Do I look like Frankenstein's wife?"

"Hardly." He let his gaze linger on her face, with her sapphire eyes sitting in pools of black. "You look beautiful."

She looked away. "Liar."

"It's true." He reached for her hand and tugged her against him, wrapping his arm around her.

After a moment, she whispered, "Are you really falling in love with me?"

"Does it matter?" In truth, he'd always been a little bit in love with her.

She shoved away from him, fixing her attention on the soft steam rising from the burnt land. "We needed rain."

"Elizabeth, you made yourself clear. You're leaving. You're not contagious, but you're not kissing me or anyone else. Don't feel bad—"

She flew against him, lassoing her arms around his neck, and pressed her lips to his cheek, up to his eye, then down to his jawline. He pulled her onto his lap and returned her affection, kissing her chin, then down her neck to the edge of her collarbone peeking above the neckline of her T-shirt.

He breathed her in—the subtle, wild fragrance of her skin and the scent of her hair that was like the rain—and sank into a moment he hoped would never end.

But as fast as she moved into him, she jumped up, stepping into the cabin of the fire tower. "I wish it would rain again. I'm burning up."

"Elizabeth—" Ryder reached for her. "Do you love me too?"

"No, I can't. Even if I did, I'm still going." She broke free and leaned against the far side of the cabin's half wall. "I'm sorry, I shouldn't have done"—she pointed to his face—"that."

"I'm not sorry. That was a pretty great kiss."

She laughed and turned to him. "I'm not sure anyone else would think so."

"But I do."

She sobered. "It changes nothing."

"Yeah, but it's good to know you love me."

She exhaled and looked over at the burnt spruce trees. "Yeah, I think I do."

Things changed after that rainy kiss. Elizabeth lowered her walls, and as they worked on the fire tower Saturday, Ryder kissed her cheek anytime he wanted. Never mind that it only deepened the hum on his lips and the ache to taste hers.

Once she leaned to kiss his cheek as he looked up to ask for more pine board, and their lips almost collided. He was so startled he shot a nail into the tower floor, barely missing his foot. Warning: Don't hold a nail gun when you might accidentally kiss the lips of the woman you love.

Sunday, he awoke with a tug to go to church. The aftermath of the fire reminded him that Someone greater than he lived.

Ryder arrived late—Fred and Ginger had decided to play hide-and-seek when he let them out—and Jeff Simmons met him in the foyer with a bulletin, then led him to a seat next to his cousin.

"Elizabeth," he said with a curt nod, sitting straight as if being in the cloud of her gentle, fragrant scent didn't mess with him.

"Ryder," she said, mimicking his tone, then laughing softly, bumping his shoulder. The air between them had definitely changed.

After church, Granny D. invited him home for lunch. He stayed through dinner and a family game of Catan, grateful for every minute in Elizabeth's presence.

Monday, he met her for dinner at Ella's. Tuesday

morning, she flew out of Nashville for Philly. Call him crazy, but he felt it the moment she lifted off.

Now he drove back from the Mace Bluff Recreation Area—someone had spotted a six-foot snake—and after relocating the fella, he headed into town for some lunch. A sandwich from Java Jane's sounded good.

As he parked, his attention fell on a new old shop in town. Earth-n-Treasures. The previous owners, the Marshalls, had retired years back, and the shop sat dark and alone. But it looked like someone had brought it back to life.

Curious, Ryder wanted to see inside. The Marshalls used to sell antique jewelry as well as their own designs. Perhaps Jewell did the same.

A bell rang as he entered. The shop smelled of paint and new lumber, and the hardwood floor had been refinished. Walking along the display cases, a diamond in a silver or platinum setting with some kind of fancy design caught his eye.

"You have good taste." A woman about his mother's age came from the back room, drying her hands on a large apron. She wore no makeup, and her grayish-blonde hair was knotted on top of her head. Ryder liked her. "It's an antique platinum ring with a scroll border. The diamond is a two-carat oval cut."

Ryder whistled low. "It's beautiful."

"Like the girl you love?"

Ryder glanced up, catching Jewell's eye, feeling as if she knew everything about him. "Yeah, but she's in Pennsylvania right now looking at grad school."

"I'm Jewell," she said, offering her hand.

"Ryder Donovan."

"Let me give you a closer look." Jewell unlocked the case and passed him the ring, saying something about it being a century old.

But Ryder only heard half of what she said, since his nerves fired on all cylinders and his pulse thumped through his ears. What was he doing holding an engagement ring?

Jewell handed him a loupe to examine this near-flawless diamond's clarity and quality, and for the next fifteen minutes, Ryder learned everything he needed to know about the stone, the platinum setting, and how its previous owner was passionately loved by her husband. Then he handed it back.

"No?" Jewell said. "You don't think she'd love this ring?"

"I'm afraid she doesn't really love me enough to accept it."

Jewell gave a nod of understanding and returned the ring to its case. "I hope it's here when you *do* need it."

"More like *if* I ever need it. At least with this girl."

"Do you want to know the price? Just in case?"

"Not really." Ryder backed toward the door. "Good luck with your shop. I'm glad this space is up and running again."

"Come in anytime."

He walked through the sun and heat of a late afternoon to Java Jane's. He ordered a Cuban sandwich and a large sweet tea. Choosing a booth by the window, he watched Hearts Bend hustle past, the cool texture of the diamond ring still on his fingertips.

———— ❤ ————

Elizabeth had walked the red brick paths of Shoemaker Green, visited residence halls and libraries. The Penn Museum Library was her favorite. From the Starbucks at 1920 Commons, she purchased a latte and cinnamon scone, then chatted with some students who raved about the university, especially Wharton—the world's first collegiate school of business—and the Wharton Way.

By the time she made her way across campus to the Steinberg Hall–Dietrich Hall admin building, she was energized. Visiting had been the right thing. She had a definitive answer for Granny. This was in her heart, not just her head.

And today was the perfect midsummer day. A light breeze brushed through the campus of large, lush trees. The temperature was warm but without the thickness of central Tennessee's humidity. It reminded her of summers at home in Boston. And she loved it.

Her phone buzzed from her crossbody bag with a text from Will. She opened the video to see him with Ethan and Jeff on the back deck of Pop's Yer Uncle, working on triple-scoop ice-cream cones. They waved, hollering, "We miss you."

Then the phone panned to the right and Ryder sat on the edge of the picnic table bench, tall cone in hand, giving Will and his video a slight nod and a short wave.

When the video ended, she lowered her phone, feeling all her Wharton zeal drain away. She batted away the mist in her eyes and caught sight of a bronze statue of Benjamin Franklin reading a newspaper while sitting on a bench.

"Hey, Ben," Elizabeth said, dropping down next to him. "Nice school you got here." She patted his bronze knee. "Me? I'm a Wharton candidate, waiting to be admitted." She listened to the breeze for a moment. "Nothing is wrong. Well, honestly, I was having a great day until my cousin sent a video of two other cousins and a friend. A close friend." She zipped up the one-sided conversation as a block of students passed, then continued once they were out of earshot. "The video…I mean, those guys are like my brothers. And I have a real brother. They said they missed me, and I know it's more teasing than anything, but I can't help but feel like they're trying to bend my will to theirs."

She paused to breathe. "They want me to join the family business. We make fine furniture. Yet, I'm kind of jealous. I wish I was having ice cream with them. Can you believe it? I'm sitting with Ben Franklin on the beautiful UPenn campus, a stone's throw from the Wharton School, and I'm longing for a chocolate sea salt caramel ice-cream cone from Pop's Yer Uncle in Hearts Bend, Tennessee. Who does that?" She glanced at Ben as if expecting an answer. "Yeah, it does seem like I'm the one who does that. What?" She leaned toward the statue. "Is it more than cousins and ice cream? I don't know… maybe."

No maybe. For sure, it was Ryder. Seeing him there with a drop of sunlight on his dark hair, polishing a few strands to a burnished red. She'd never noticed the firm line of his jaw the way she did in the video. Or how much he said with one glance of his brown eyes. Why didn't he give her a goofy smile and wave like Ethan and Jeff? He acted like he couldn't care less.

They'd had a great weekend together working on the fire tower, where their lips almost met. She flushed at the memory. Then he stayed at Granny and Pops's all day after church. He pitched in with after-dinner cleanup and helped Pops carry fresh wood out to his workshop with Will.

Cousin Bobby's wife, Mila, cornered Elizabeth after lunch, wanting to know her checklist for her Wharton visit. Mila was a lot like Julie. While Julie was classically down-to-earth, Mila carried an easy, elegant sophistication.

It was all Elizabeth could do not to tell her the truth. *I'm going to persuade the admin office to move me off the wait-list.*

Instead, she said, "I have to nail down where I'm going to live."

They ended up online looking at the campus and the surrounding area. Mila texted a friend of hers about housing and passed on the info to Elizabeth.

Yet the entire time, Pops and Granny, Bobby and Ethan, cousins Jen and Kate, talked around them about the rest of the summer in Hearts Bend and how excited they were for fall and Rock Mill High football. Plans were starting for the October Festival, and Granny said at least ten times how colorful downtown was when the leaves turned gold and red.

There was talk of another barbecue on the back deck and a birthday party for Aunt Meryl, who turned sixty this year. Dad and Mom were secretly coming to surprise her. Which was news to Elizabeth. But she was going to miss all of it.

For the first time, she caught a glimpse of what Granny and Pops tried to tell her. The Dorseys were a unit knit together in this glorious thing called family. It wasn't meant to stifle her but to accept and love her. Maybe even protect her.

Then Ryder walked by after Mila left their conversation and the picnic table to join a game of cornhole, and he seemed to be the missing piece of the puzzle she was mentally piecing together. To be honest, she was so confused after dinner with him Monday night, she was glad to wing away Tuesday morning.

"I'd better go, Ben," she said. "I have an appointment at two. Wish me luck." She hesitated before rising to her feet. "Any advice?"

The statue said nothing, of course—if it did, she might be crazy—but something in the breeze stirred words from a verse Pops used to say.

"The Lord…will give you the desires of your heart."

"Fred, Ginger, your beloved master is home." Ryder tossed his keys into the bowl on the kitchen counter as deep barks echoed through the house. Setting down his sacks from Cooper's Grocery, he wrestled with the pups on the cool kitchen tile, then let them out to stretch and do their business.

Filling their bowls with food, he wondered what he'd done with the spaghetti sauce recipe given to him by Isobel, his favorite nanny. She always made spaghetti on cold nights, but on this summer evening, he had a taste for home. Sunday with the Dorseys reminded him of why he came home in the first place. His parents may not be around much, but everyone else who embraced and raised him lived in Hearts Bend.

In fact, Pops Dorsey invited him to a five a.m. men's gathering tomorrow morning. "Do a bit of praying. Read a bit of the Word." He'd slapped Ryder on the back. "Make a better man out of you."

Ryder put away the groceries, threw in a load of laundry, and collected the mail. He checked the pine in his workshop and decided he had enough to finish the fire tower. After a quick shower, he flipped on all the kitchen lights to make the sauce. If he couldn't find the recipe, he'd work from memory. He knew the most important ingredients: tomato sauce, tomatoes, garlic, and lean ground beef.

He'd just set the meat to browning when he noticed a small white box in the corner of the kitchen counter. It was tied with a red ribbon, but there was no tag or label. Nothing written on the bottom. Pulling the box from the bow, he raised the lid to see another one inside. He glanced around as if someone might spring from a hiding place.

Where did this—

He opened it to see the diamond ring from Earth-n-Treasures. What? He snapped it closed and tossed it onto the counter.

Was someone trying to frame him? First, the WMA fraud. And now this? He yanked his phone from his pocket and searched for the shop's number. But he could only find the old one from when the Marshalls owned the place. Close enough.

"Come on, Jewell, answer." But the phone simply rang and rang. When he hung up, he snapped off the heat under the browning meat, tied on his sneakers, and headed out. He was taking this ring back. Now.

But as he stepped onto his deck, his parents were climbing up the stairs.

"Mom, Dad, what are you doing here?" He snatched a

barking Fred's collar, then a barking Ginger's. His parents weren't pet people.

"We cut our trip short," Dad said. "We thought we'd come into town, check on the house, and see our hero son."

"Karl?" Ryder said, referencing his older brother with a short laugh.

"No, you." Mom patted him on the shoulder as she stepped into the kitchen. "The place looks nice, Ryder. Who'd you hire for the work?"

"I did it myself, Mom." He dragged the dogs off to his room, then returned to the wide, bright living room with the bank of windows on both sides.

"You didn't learn that from me," Dad said.

Pops D. taught Ryder almost everything he knew about carpentry, electrical, and plumbing.

"How long are you in town?" Ryder tucked the white box back in the corner of the kitchen and offered his parents bottles of water. "I'm making Isobel's spaghetti sauce. Care to join me?"

"We're on a vegan diet," Mom said. "But thank you. Next time."

"So, how have you all been?" He'd not seen them in a while, but they texted. Called.

"Good but busy." Dad, dressed in fine-weave slacks and a starched shirt, inspected the rest of the house with the soft strike of his handcrafted shoes against the hardwoods.

Mom read something on her phone. She was pretty in a summer dress and sandals, her hair worked into a braid with a bit of gray peeking through the blonde.

"So, how was the celebration?" Dad said, returning to

the main room. "We read about it in the *Tribune* online. We're sorry we missed it."

"You know how Hearts Bend does these things. All the way." Ryder was torn between welcoming his parents and running the ring back to Earth-n-Treasures. He had a gut feeling the next folks at his door would be the police.

After some small talk, Mom suggested dinner at Valentino's. "If you're hungry for spaghetti, Ry, we can go there. Valentino's has vegan options."

"All right, if you want. Let me change." He ducked into his room for jeans, a white button-down, and a pair of black leather sneakers. Valentino's was upscale Italian, where pro football players like Sam Hardy hung out when they were in town. "Ready?" he said, exiting his room.

He wasn't hungry for just spaghetti. He was hungry for Isobel's sauce and a taste of his childhood. Funny, though, how his parents showed up when he was feeling a bit nostalgic. It was good to see them. Also, Earth-n-Treasures was around the corner from Valentino's.

"I'll drive," Dad said, always in charge.

"I'll take my truck. You won't have to bring me back." Ryder grabbed his keys, jerking around at a knock on the door. This was the moment. The police had arrived.

But it was Elizabeth. Smiling. Hands twisted together. "Hey," she said.

"You're back." He gave her a slightly reserved hug. But when she hugged him back, he wrapped her tight in his arms. "How was it?"

"Ryder?" Mom's voice floated over his shoulder. "Who's this?"

Elizabeth released him, jerking backward. "Hello," she said.

"This is Elizabeth Dorsey. Elizabeth, meet my parents. Graham and Cherry Donovan."

She glanced between Ryder and his parents as if assessing the situation, then smiled and shook their hands, saying how nice it was to meet them.

"She's been visiting Wharton, checking out the campus."

"Impressive," Dad said. "We'd have liked Ryder to take a more traditional path, but—"

"Ryder didn't want to, did he?" Ryder said. Then to Elizabeth, "We're going to Valentino's. Come with us."

"No, no, I, um, can't." She was still twisting her hands together. "I just came by to—" Ryder leaned close. To what? "It was nice to meet you, Mr. and Mrs. Donovan." She exited the deck in a hurry.

"Beth?" Ryder chased after her down the steps and across the driveway to where she'd parked her Bug. "You okay? What's going on?"

She turned to him. "Nothing." Her wide, white smile hid her lie. Something was wrong. "I should go. I told Tina I'd cover for her tonight. She's got a chance to do some granny duty." She patted his chest. "We'll catch up later."

"And Wharton?"

"Absolutely fantastic." Her tone didn't match her words. "I chatted with Ben Franklin."

As she drove off, Dad walked by with Mom, saying they'd meet Ryder at the restaurant. Back at the house, he released the dogs from his room, tossed them a treat, shoved the browning meat into the fridge, grabbed the white box with the red ribbon, and locked up.

He parked on Blossom Street in the shade of the historic Wedding Shop, then cut through a couple of yards and parking lots to Earth-n-Treasures.

On approach, he could see the windows white with light. The bell rang when he opened the door. A man came from the back.

"Can I help you? We're about to close."

"Is Jewell here?" Ryder set the box on the glass counter.

"Jewell? We *have* jewels..." He chuckled at his comment, then sobered. "Sorry, there's no one named Jewell here."

"She showed me this ring yesterday." Ryder pushed the box toward the man, who opened it and examined the ring under a loupe.

"It's a nice piece. The shank is antique, the stone nearly flawless." He handed the ring back to Ryder. "We didn't have that ring in our inventory. I'd remember."

"What? It was in this case right here." Ryder tapped on the glass. "Are you seriously telling me you don't know this ring?"

"You say you bought it here?"

"I didn't buy it. I just looked at it."

"Then why do you have it?"

"That's what I'd like to know. I'm bringing it back."

"Well, I can't afford to pay you for it. We're just getting started. I'd have to research, see how much it's worth."

"It was in this case." Ryder tapped the glass once more. What world had he stepped into? "I'm *returning* it."

"You can't return what wasn't ours. I'd have to buy it from you."

"But I didn't buy it."

"I don't know what to tell you." The man regarded Ryder as if he might be a little loony. "Maybe this Jewell made a gift of it. Is she a friend?"

"No. I've only seen her the one time. When I walked in here."

"It's just my wife and me. Her name is Vivi. We just leased the place. It's been empty for years. We finished painting last week."

"So there's no Jewell?"

"Afraid not."

Ryder snatched up the ring box. "Well, if you discover a Jewell, call me." He tossed his business card on the case. "Thanks."

Stepping outside into the warm evening, the ring box burning in his hand, Ryder boiled with confusion and something like anger. What was going on? Was someone after him? What was he supposed to do with this ring? Report it to the police?

Or, and this idea was the first to bring a sliver of peace, did he admit he'd just encountered something Divine?

How many times had she walked through the kitchen door to see Granny, and sometimes Pops, wrapped in an apron, stirring up something for dinner? Hundreds if she counted all her summer and family holidays.

"Don't tell me you're working at Ella's," Granny said. "I made meatloaf with mashed potatoes and green beans and my homemade cherry popover for dinner."

"Got the night off. Hang on, I'll be down to help." Elizabeth ran upstairs, kicking off her shoes the moment she entered her room and dropping her bag on her bed.

It'd been almost a week since she returned from Wharton. She willed herself not to check her email every five minutes. But her meeting with the administration had gone well. Very well. In fact, the dean of admissions came by and joined the conversation. She was good friends with one of Elizabeth's recommending MIT professors. She also knew an associate of Dad's and was a huge Patriots fan. Thanks to her brother Jonathan, Elizabeth was a wealth of Patriots and Tom Brady knowledge.

By the time she headed back to her hotel, she felt in her soul she'd have an acceptance by the end of the week.

Changing into shorts and a T-shirt, she wrapped her hair in a topknot and sat at her computer. Through a narrowed gaze, she checked email.

Junk and ads were followed by group emails from her MIT friends. She deleted most of them and was about to go down to the kitchen when a new email dropped in. From Wharton.

Dear Elizabeth,

Congratulations on your acceptance—

Trembling, she fired out of her chair, knocking it into her bed. She was in. She was in. Elizabeth leaned over the desk to read the letter again, savoring every delicious word.

She was accepted. She was a Whartonite. She jigged about her room. Two years from now, she'd have an MBA from one of the finest universities in the world.

The letter said they valued her application. Said it showed her commitment to knowledge, tenacity, and to others.

She was in! Thundering down the stairs, she ran into Pops, who folded his weekly paper.

"Pops, I'm in. I got in!" She hugged him so hard he had to steady himself with a hand on the wall. "Granny, I'm in. They accepted me. I knew visiting campus would do it." She broke off a corner from a slice of meatloaf. "Bless Jonathan for all his useless football knowledge."

"Wait, what?" Pops looked up from setting the kitchen table. "I thought you were in."

"I was wait-listed."

"Why didn't you tell us?" Granny said.

"Because…" The thrill of her acceptance faded a bit. "I wanted to be positive. I didn't want you all to feel sorry for me."

"We would've prayed for you," Pops said.

"And I guess I thought maybe you'd tell me I wasn't meant to go." She glanced from Pops to Granny, realizing how much she'd judged them. "You'd pressure me to stay here. Work at Dorsey."

"I'm sorry you felt that way, Beth." Granny's embrace was sweet and fragrant, like her kitchen, like her life. "Sorry if we made you feel like we didn't support you."

"Yeah, kiddo," Pops said. "We're Team Elizabeth all the way."

Granny leaned back to see Elizabeth's face, her expression full of love. "However, we are going to miss you. Matt, get on the horn. Call everyone over. Let's have a party for our girl. When do you leave for real since you actually got accepted?"

"First-year students need to be there on August fifth for pre-term exercises." She glanced at her smartwatch. "I have to leave this weekend. Or before. Mila's friend has a studio apartment, recently updated. She said if I got in I could have it at a discount."

Suddenly, it all felt a bit overwhelming, and she battled the familiar rise of semester anxiety. What if she got sick again? No, she wouldn't. Just no. She was supposed to be calm, cool, and collected. An educated woman who knew how to function under pressure.

"Sit and eat. We'll talk," Granny said. "Matt, maybe we should wait on the celebration—"

"No, it's fine." Elizabeth moved the mashed potatoes to the table. "If we're going to celebrate, tonight is the night."

She'd have to tell Will that Friday was her last day. No, Thursday. She should pack up Friday, drive a couple of hours, then stop for the night. She trembled with the weight of it all.

"I have to tell Tina," she said, reaching for her phone. "She scheduled me all day Saturday. But I can't delay or I risk not being set for pre-term exercises."

"I agree," Granny said. She smiled when she faced Elizabeth, but there was a soft sadness in her response. "I'll help with your laundry. Maybe we can run to Sheffield's for linens and dishes, whatever else you might need in your apartment. Oh, a lovely piece of art. Maybe a plant." She set a platter of sliced meatloaf on the table along with a pitcher of iced tea.

"A shopping spree on Pops and me. To get you started."

"I'll tell the kids to bring something for her new place. Something to remember us all." Pops whipped out his phone and tapped the screen like a pro.

"Oh, Granny, Pops." Elizabeth fell against her grandmother. "Thank you."

In the middle of Granny's delicious dinner—which Elizabeth barely tasted, she was so wound up—she told her grandparents about the apartment in Rittenhouse Square with a great view of the park and a twenty-minute walk to Wharton.

The more she talked about campus and the courses, the more she knew this was the right direction. The knot in the middle of her chest eased up a bit.

But she had work to finish at Dorsey. And she hated leaving Tina in a lurch. Then there was Ryder.

After dinner, she headed back to her room to call her parents, who volunteered to bring over more clothes and some personal items on the sixteenth. Dad, as promised, transferred money for the first semester.

Then she made lists of everything, from Dorsey tasks to things she might want from Sheffield's. The last thing she wrote before Julie and Mila called her down to "get this party started" was *Take pictures of the fire tower at sunset.*

19

"Guess it's my turn to say congratulations." Ryder sat on the picnic table under twin maples near where they'd danced the night of the guitar pull.

Elizabeth glanced over at him. "Will you miss me?"

"Yes, will you miss me?" They'd not talked much since her sorta-maybe confession of love.

"You know I will."

A low fire burned in the stone firepit, and music played from speakers mounted on the side of the house. On the other side of the trees, Will and Markey played bocce ball with Ethan and Bobby.

Officer-cousin Jeff stopped by long enough for congratulations and a large piece of Haven's Bakery cake. His girlfriend Ursula had arrived about an hour ago and was on the deck with Mila, Julie, Beka, and Granny D.

"How was dinner with your parents?" Elizabeth said to Ryder after a moment.

"Nice. I got a full update on their lives. One thing

about my parents, they never change. Everything revolves around their careers."

"I understand that." Elizabeth picked up a dying leaf and tore away the edges.

"Dad grew up old-school. Worked hard, got a good education, and strived for the top. His great-grandparents emigrated to the US as kids during the Irish Potato Famine, and I'm not sure the poverty mentality ever left them. Mom grew up with money, but her parents told her to never depend on anyone but herself. Not her husband, or friends, or children. She was a National Merit Scholar and wrote her own ticket."

"I'm surprised you fell for me," Elizabeth said. "I sound a lot like your mom."

"Maybe that's why I fell for you."

"Because you missed your mom during childhood, and I'm the substitute? How Freudian of you." Elizabeth let the last of the leaf in her hand flutter to the ground.

"No, I meant I really admire and respect Mom."

"But you still wish she'd been around more."

Was she fishing for something beyond Ryder's childhood? Like a peek into her future through Ryder's view of his mother? "Doesn't every kid?"

"We're not talking about every kid."

A couple more Dorsey cousins, aunts, and uncles arrived, pausing to hug Elizabeth and hand over something from their personal belongings. The picnic table was stacked with towels, boxes, decorative pillows, framed family photos, pots, pans, knickknacks, a carefully bagged quilt someone said belonged to Great-Granny, and envelopes, which Ryder guessed contained money.

"Mom was around more with my brother," he said when they were alone again. "I was the surprise caboose baby, and her career was a freight train. She did provide the best care and education. Keeping me here in Hearts Bend when moving to Nashville or Atlanta would've been easier for them."

"All fear of passing on Epstein–Barr aside, you're making my case on why I'm not so keen on marriage. I don't want my kid saying the same things about me in thirty years."

"I think there's a balance to it all, Beth. In the end, it comes down to priorities and values. I sometimes wonder if my mom regrets being away so much. She hinted at it during dinner when she asked me about you."

"Me? What did you tell her?"

He looked into her eyes for a moment, then toward the bocce game. "That you were a Dorsey and I knew you from the summers you worked at Ella's. I said you were a friend, also smart, ambitious, determined, fun, easy to laugh with and"—he glanced at her again—"beautiful. To which my mom agreed."

Each confession warmed her, filling places in her she didn't know were empty. She liked to believe a career-minded, independent woman was not wooed by a man's words, but she'd take them. Treasure them.

"Oh, hey, any word from the Colorado offer?" she said.

"Naw. I'm not going. Travis called me into his office this afternoon, apologized again for the misunderstanding, and talked about my career with the WMA. I think he wants to move up and hand me his job."

"That's quite a turnaround. Congratulations. I think

Will still wants me to take Dan Harper's place when he retires in three years? Stay at Dorsey, work with Dan, become CFO when he leaves." She nudged Ryder's shoulder. "By the way, Travis is right. You'd be good in his job."

"Maybe you can come back to Dorsey after your master's degree."

She laughed softly. "Probably not, but we'll see."

"I wish you all the best, Beth." Ryder kissed her cheek. It was clinical and cold, not like the passionate ones he whispered along her jaw and down her neck that night at the fire tower. The mere memory made her shiver. "When do you leave?"

"Thursday afternoon. I'll drive halfway."

Ryder slid off the picnic table. "Don't be a stranger. Come visit."

"You know I will." The exchange was perfunctory. They both knew it'd be a long time before she returned to Hearts Bend.

He glanced toward the family, some playing games, some gathered by the smoldering firepit, talking and laughing. "You should go celebrate with everyone."

As he walked away, Elizabeth felt...what? Cold? As if something had been taken from her. She ran after him. "Ryder?"

"Yeah?" He turned slowly, and in the dusky light she caught a shimmer in his eyes.

"I'll text you."

He nodded once. "Sure."

Sure? Nothing about this moment contained the affection she'd grown to love about their relationship. But what did she expect? He'd told her he loved her. She told him she was leaving.

As she joined the family breaking out the goodies for s'mores, she fought a familiar sensation. The one she'd battled every summer as a teen on her last day in Hearts Bend—that this place was home and she could not go a single day without seeing Ryder Donovan.

♥

After leaving Dorsey on Wednesday with a small box from her office, Elizabeth returned her shirts and apron to Ella's. Tina sat in her corner booth, eating a chef salad and going over the monthly accounts on her laptop.

"So, you're really leaving," she said, scootching her work aside, giving Elizabeth her full attention. "I know, I know, you were never going to be a permanent face at Ella's—I saw your star rising when you were a teenager. It's just now I realize that final day has come. Shoot, I thought I'd lost you for good when you headed to MIT, but you worked a couple of weeks your freshman summer. And I snagged you for a couple of Christmas breaks."

"You're going to make me cry." Elizabeth motioned for Lucy to bring her a Diet Coke. "I'm grateful to you, Tina. You taught me a lot. And you trusted me."

"I'd sell the place to you if I thought it'd make you happy."

Elizabeth laughed softly as she reached for a napkin to catch the single tear in the corner of her eye. "You sound like Will. Wanting me to be CFO."

"You're a talent, Beth. You're good with people. You're clever and intuitive. Wharton is lucky to get you. Blow their socks off, hmmm? And if one of those fancy Fortune 100 companies like Goldman Sachs doesn't hire you, they're fools. Just remember you are far more than anything you put on a résumé."

"I'm not that great, Tina, but I'll take the compliment."

"You are. You went to Wharton and won over the admin thingamajig! That's you being you." Tina stabbed at her salad. "Next time, don't lie to us about your future." Elizabeth heard that lecture over and over.

Tina went on, talking about the diner and how Buck Mathews mentioned Ella's during an interview that was just published, and the phone's been ringing off the hook. Elizabeth listened with yearning as she talked about *Inside NashVegas* coming to do a piece on the diner. "And on me, Tina Danner, how about that?"

"You'll be great," Elizabeth said, again with the sensation of missing out. As if she was letting go of something she loved. "Text me when it airs."

"So," Tina began, sitting back, sipping her iced tea. "How did you leave things with Ryder?"

"Same as always. Hello, goodbye, stay in touch."

Tina made a face. "He loves you. I can tell by the look on his face."

"He told me."

Tina sat forward, dropping her glass to the table with a thud. "And what did you say?"

"I don't know…Nothing." Tina knew about the Epstein–Barr as it pertained to food safety, but perhaps not about kissing. "I can't let him kiss me or anything. What if I'm infectious and don't know it?"

"What? You didn't kiss him because you *might* be

infectious? But you're not infectious. Otherwise, you'd not be in my kitchen."

"I know, I know, but—"

"You used it as an excuse?"

"And a pretty darn good one."

Tina let a long sigh be her reply. "I never met anyone who fought love so hard."

"I'm not fighting. I'm staying focused."

"I know, and I just praised you for it. However, I'm a sucker for love. Yes to Wharton and a big fancy job, but make room for love, Beth. Don't be the woman who loses herself to a big fancy job that requires all her time, energy, and heart. No one wants to go home to a beautiful apartment with big windows overlooking city lights and eat alone."

"I'll go to dinner with friends."

"You mean colleagues and you'll talk work all night."

"So? That's how I grow, learn, network."

"Okay, okay. I'm team Beth. But..." Tina yanked a napkin from the caddy and shoved it toward Elizabeth. Then she took a pen from her pocket.

When does love get a chance?

Fine. Elizabeth grabbed the pen and wrote on the napkin.

When I'm thirty-two.

She turned the napkin to Tina.

"Sign it," Tina said.

"Sign it? Are we making a contract?"

Tina tapped the napkin with her finger. "Yes. Sign it."

Elizabeth shook her head, laughing, and penned her name across the bottom. "There. Happy? It's not binding, you know."

"Of course it is." Tina tucked the napkin under her laptop and took a bite of her salad. "Girl, when I met my husband, I was a goner." She patted her heart. "Nothing mattered but him. We rushed down the aisle, had three boys—bam, bam, bam—while he built a great construction business. He's the one who told me Ella's was being sold, if not closing. Together we figured out a way to buy it. He wanted it to be all mine. Little did I know he was going to be arrested by the FBI for fraud a few years later. But he knew enough about his dealings to keep them from taking this place."

"Have you ever let love back in?" Elizabeth said, a tone of knowing in her voice. "You've been divorced for what, ten, fifteen years? What about Marty? He seems keen on—"

"We're not talking about me." Stab, stab, stab at what remained of her salad. "And for your information, I have agreed to dinner with Marty. But we're just friends." She jabbed her fork at Elizabeth. "You'll be at school by then."

"I want photographic evidence."

"You won't be dancing at my wedding anytime soon, but sweetheart, I hope to be dancing at yours."

"Why do you care so much?" Elizabeth said. "Your marriage didn't turn out so great. How do I know Ryder won't commit fraud or cheat on me or die? Love is not without risk."

"Everything is a risk. School. Work. Love. Life. If I hadn't fallen in love and married, I'd not have the boys:

Cole, Chris, and Cap. My grandchildren. My husband was a good man who made a big mistake, and he paid for it. He's remarried now. Doing well." Tina slid from the booth with her salad bowl and empty tea glass. "Do me a favor. If you have any feelings for Ryder Donovan, keep in touch. You may think thirty-two is the right time to pursue love, but men like Ryder Donovan don't come along every day."

20

Ryder hauled the last of the pine to the fire tower as Elizabeth drove out of town. He paused every few boards for a drink of water and to stare over the charred, barren landscape.

Today, the view felt like his life. Not to play the melodramatic card or "poor me"—he'd had enough of that as a kid—but losing Elizabeth hurt.

He'd put himself out there. Told her he loved her. Right in this very spot where he nailed boards. Where future WMA officers would look for fires. Or newly engaged couples would carve their initials.

In this square box, he'd shared the most amazing kiss ever, not involving lip-to-lip contact.

Ryder glanced again toward the burnt area. An early-morning rain made everything look shiny, but the afternoon's hot August sun drank up all the moisture.

By evening, he'd placed the last board on the tower and stood back, the fresh pine filling his senses.

As he packed up his tools, Dad called. Was Ryder free

for dinner? Mom was heading out of town in the morning, and Dad had a golfing weekend set up with Karl and a couple of friends.

"You're welcome to join us. It's a course in Wisconsin. Lovely this time of year."

"Thanks, Dad. I'm not much of a golfer."

"No, I guess not. I never could get you to see the point of it."

"But dinner sounds nice."

"Invite your friend. The Dorsey girl."

"She left today." He settled the cordless nail gun into the case, then gathered the rest of the tools. "Headed to Wharton."

"Good for her."

"What time for dinner, Dad?"

"Seven. Your mom had an urge to make her beef Wellington."

Mom's Christmas dish. It was one of Ryder's favorite memories of her, in the kitchen, wrapped in a big apron, making a mess with pots and pans, and a mixer, declaring she was never "doing this again." But the house was always so fragrant. And the beef Wellington was so good, Ryder wrote a school essay about it.

"Hey, Dad," Ryder said. "Before you go, I've received a job offer from my old boss. In Colorado. Do you think I should take it?"

"Does it help your career? Do you want to live in Colorado? Are there socioeconomic reasons?"

"I have friends. I'd work for my old boss, and the job would be a promotion, but in a completely different park system. I like Colorado. But being in Hearts Bend feels right."

"Sometimes we have to make the tough decisions to get ahead. Staying home is lovely if you can do it. But do what you think is best."

"Thanks, Dad," Ryder said. "I'll see you at seven."

"Wait, Ryder," Dad said. "Let me say I've learned over the years that some things are more valuable than a career and money. I know I'm late in saying it, but I'm sorry I wasn't around more when you were a kid."

Surprised by his father's raw honesty, he felt a wave of compassion. "Dad, it's okay, I understand."

"Do what you want. What you know will make you happy. Trust that God is big enough to work in your life even with mistakes. Go with your gut."

Go with his gut? Trust God? Dad never came close to attributing anything to God or saying something like "go with your gut." Well, Ryder's gut said stay, work for the WMA. His heart hoped Elizabeth would come home, realize she belonged with him.

At his place, he played with the dogs after dinner and replayed Dad's advice. *Trust God. Go with your gut.* Ryder tossed the ball for Fred, then Ginger. As they scurried away, chasing each other more than the ball, he scooped up his phone and called Elizabeth.

When her voicemail picked up, he almost hit End, but after a panicked second and a big gulp of Tennessee air, he said, "Elizabeth, it's Ryder. I was just talking to my dad, and he said I should go with my gut—which if you knew him *at all*, he'd never say that—but here goes. I know you're on your way to Wharton, but I love you. With my whole heart. I want to marry you. Now, or next year, or when you graduate, or after a year into your career. You tell me. But I'm asking you to marry me, Elizabeth Dorsey. What do you say? Will you?"

———— ♥ ————

Elizabeth stared at her laptop screen and the horizontal line of her pre-exercise term paper. It was due at 11:59 p.m. She had five hundred crummy words of a thousand. At this rate, all one thousand would be crummy. She used to knock these projects out in her sleep—hyperbole, but you get it—and turn them in early. But this time, her mind was fuzzy and everything felt hard.

She tapped the face of her phone for the time. 10:15. She went back to staring at the partially blank page.

The assignment—to analyze a previous work situation prior to arriving at Wharton—took all of her time between research, group discussions, watching lectures, and organizing it all into this paper.

Since arriving at Wharton, she'd had a few calls with her parents. One with Granny. Answered texts from Tina. Hopped on a video call with Will and Dan to go over the accounting system she'd recommended. Otherwise, her life was lived between campus and her very cozy Rittenhouse Square apartment.

Grabbing her notepad, where she'd scribbled thoughts and a high-level structure for her assignment, she tried to find the inspiration to finish this project. Time was ticking.

After a minute, she got up, crashed on the loveseat, and opened the voice message she'd listened to a dozen times.

"Elizabeth, it's Ryder." She rested the phone on her chest and listened. "I was just talking to my dad…go with my gut…I want to marry you." Elizabeth closed her eyes, waiting for the question. "…Will you marry me?"

When the message finished, she hit play again and wiped away the single tear sliding down her cheek.

"Will you marry me?" boomed through her every time, shaking what she believed to be her very firm foundation. Why? Why would he ask her this when he knew the answer? Worse, why was she listening to it? Again. She moved to hit Delete, but instead cradled the phone against her chest.

A kind, good, handsome man with the softest lips and the richest kisses had asked her to marry him.

Sitting up, Elizabeth tossed her phone to the other cushion. He deserved an answer. The message was three weeks old. Yes, she'd been ignoring a marriage proposal for three weeks, which was so not like her.

"You have a paper to write."

Her subject was the TWRA fraud she'd discovered over the summer. Which kept her thinking of Ryder. Ah, she felt so stuck.

Elizabeth jumped up for a bottle of water, then peered out her front window into the street, where couples with takeout headed into the apartment across the road, warm lights glowing from nearly every window.

Gathering herself, she returned to her IKEA desk (thanks, Dad) and typed another two hundred words. They weren't good words, but words nonetheless.

Then she called Will.

"Elizabeth?" he said. "Is everything all right?" He sounded drowsy…like she'd woken him up.

She glanced at her smartwatch. "Oh, Will, sorry, it's almost eleven."

"It's okay. I was finishing a book. What's up?"

"I'm working on a paper due in fifty-nine minutes."

"I remember those days." Will had his master's from Vanderbilt. "Can I help?"

"Um, no." Her voice quivered a little. "Sorry, I'm just tired. I picked the fraud case to analyze for my pre-exercise paper, and I'm not sure it's worth a thousand words. Anyway, only three hundred to go."

"Have you added your personal reflection and learning? You paid attention to things we ignored. It's why you're a good leader, Beth. Maybe pad your intro with history on Dorsey. Give an example of another fraud case."

Elizabeth came alive and scrambled for a pen.

"Then give your honest conclusion. Add in how the firm realized we had to jump on a new accounting system. Dan wrote the check for ProfitWise today. We start prepping on the first of September."

"You're going to love the system. I was part of an install team during my internship in Boston."

"I won't say 'Wish you were here to help us.'"

Why not? Worse things were said to her. Like "marry me." "How's everyone?" she said softly.

"Everyone is good. So is Ryder, in case you want to know."

"He's part of everyone, isn't he?"

"Granny asked him to lunch after church twice, and he turned her down. I think he misses you."

"Will?" she began. "He asked me to marry him."

He was silent for a few beats. "I see. When?"

"The day I left. Only, not to my face. He called and left a voice message."

"What did you tell him?"

"Nothing. I got here and got busy, you know, setting up the apartment, starting pre-exercise courses."

"No wonder he looks so miserable. Beth, you can't leave him hanging. Call him."

"I know, but I don't know what to say."

"Come on, Beth. You can't hit grad school and your career goals with guns blazing while running like a scared kitten from your personal life. From love. It makes you a woman of ambition, but not a leader. A good man asked you to marry him. You owe him the respect and honor of an answer."

"I know, I know. Argh, I feel so stupid for leaving him hanging."

"Then call him."

When she hung up, Elizabeth stared at the words on her laptop screen, wondering where the girl she used to know had gone. She'd not felt like herself since...that night Ryder walked into Ella's.

"Focus," she said, looking at her notes, then pounding out the rest of her paper, fueled by Will's bold, unabashed truth.

Then she was going to call Ryder, leave him a voice message. She'd let the replay of his question live rent-free in her head far too long.

At 11:55, she hit send on her paper. Then called Ryder. She'd leave him a message and be done with it. But he answered.

"Elizabeth."

She panicked. And did what every normal red-blooded American woman would do.

She hung up.

♥

October rolled into Hearts Bend with crisp mornings and sunny afternoons. It felt good to bid so long to the summer heat. After September's heavy rains, the burnt area of Cheatham WMA sprouted signs of life.

This afternoon, Ryder headed to Ella's for a late lunch and an optimistic order of fifty chicken baskets. Since the fire, the TWRA wanted all departments to focus on fire-safety education. Ryder was teaching at the Kids Theater every Wednesday after school.

As he circled Gardenia Park, he heard music coming from the small amphitheater. Buck Mathews, home from a summer tour, was playing tonight for his hometown.

Last time he was in the park, Ryder had just ordered chicken baskets from Ella's and stared into Elizabeth Dorsey's blue eyes. But he'd put those days and memories behind him.

Dad's advice to go with his gut was a bust. Granted, a voicemail marriage proposal might have been a bit much, but Elizabeth never responded until about a month ago.

She'd called at midnight. When he answered, she hung up. He tried to call back, but her voicemail picked up. He tried a few more times, but again, voicemail. So, he left it alone. Took the hint.

Inside Ella's, a late lunch crowd conversation buzzed

around the dining room. Ryder sat at the counter, ordering a sandwich for himself and chicken baskets for the fire-safety class.

He was reviewing his notes when Tina came from the kitchen with his lunch and her iPad. When he'd signed for the chicken basket order, she passed over the mustard and ketchup.

"So," she said, "have you heard from Elizabeth?"

"Nope."

"No one else has heard from her either." Tina gave him one of those arched-brow, how-do-you-like-them-apples looks.

"What do you mean, no one else?"

"Betty, Matt. Her cousins. Me. I mean, I know school is important and she has a lot on her plate, but surely she has a moment to say hello. You hear stories about people losing it in grad school, but I didn't think she'd be one."

"She's moved on, Tina." Ryder bit into his sandwich. It needed some mustard. He didn't want to talk about Elizabeth Dorsey. She was the past. "We should too."

"Betty called her parents, who said—" Tina gasped, staring toward the door. "Sake's alive, I don't believe it."

Ryder glanced over his shoulder to see Elizabeth standing in the light falling through large-pane windows. She wore jeans, sneakers, and a puff jacket. Soft strands of curls escaped the loose knot atop her head.

"Ryder Donovan." She all but shouted. "I need to talk to you."

———— ♥ ————

Ryder led her through the kitchen, out to the small parking lot behind Ella's. Elizabeth felt like she might implode. There were moments on the drive from Philadelphia to Hearts Bend she couldn't remember, only that she'd arrived with her heart and her head barely following.

She shouldn't have left school. But she did because she couldn't stay. She was a woman with an overwhelming dilemma. No one could help her. The answer was within.

When the exit door to the kitchen closed, she turned to Ryder. "I can't eat. Think. Sleep. I've tried to put it out of my mind, but I can't."

"Elizabeth, what are you doing here?"

"What do you think I'm doing here? Your message, Ryder. Your message. 'Will you marry me?' Remember? Did you mean it? Were you of sound mind?"

"Yes, I meant it. Yes, I was of sound mind. But—"

"You've changed your mind?" The air in the parking lot behind the diner was warm with the stench of a car engine and an overflowing dumpster. But she'd rather be here than anywhere else. "I'm too late?"

"Beth, you hung up on me. Never answered my calls."

"I know, I know. Because I was scared." They circled each other, fighters in a ring.

"Of me?"

"Of my answer." She glanced toward a noise to see Tina, Lucy, and D'Angelo stacked up, watching through a crack in the door. "So," she said to Ryder, "did you mean it?"

"Of course I meant it," he said. "Is that why you're here?"

Elizabeth broke the tension with a light laugh and leaned against Tina's car. "Ridiculous, right? I ignore you for two months, then *bam*, I show up loaded for bear, demanding to know if you meant it."

"Then *bam*, I'm here for it." He leaned against the hood of Tina's SUV. "Talk to me, Dorsey."

Elizabeth sighed as she pulled the tie from her hair so her curls fell free. She raised her gaze toward the October sky.

"First-year students had to write a paper analyzing a work situation we experienced before arriving at Wharton. I chose the TWRA fraud. Man, I was going to knock out the assignment in a week. I dove into research, listened to the lectures, studied coursework, sat in discussions." She peered at Ryder. "I didn't listen to your message for several days. I didn't want to be distracted. Didn't want the pull of your voice, of Hearts Bend. I didn't want the pull of *you*. I'd made it to Wharton, and I loved it. At least, that's what I kept telling myself. Then, when curiosity got the better of me, I listened. You asked me to marry you, and from that point on, I couldn't...I wasn't...me. I bought a bridal magazine from a newspaper stand, Ryder. A bridal magazine. I've never even been remotely interested in bridal magazines."

"Did you see anything you liked?"

Many, *many* things. "Then I started reading engagement stories online. I could write a book, I read so many. I daydreamed about proposals and weddings during my classes." She looked over at him. "What other women received a romantic voicemail proposal like me? I tried to forget, put it all behind me. My professor loved my paper on the TWRA fraud case, so I doubled down on my commitment. Until one day, when I was at lunch with my fellow students and one of them asked about my plans after Wharton, I said, 'Um, what?' I wasn't even listening to the conversation. I was thinking about a gown I really loved in *Brides* magazine."

"Elizabeth, do you want to marry me?" Ryder slipped his hand into hers.

"Yes, Ryder, as much as it pains me to say." She squeezed his hand, grinning. But he remained somber.

"Don't joke. I'm serious. If you want to finish school, I'll wait. I'll go where your career goes. I can get a job easily enough."

"That's just it, Ryder, I don't want to finish school." She peered into his eyes, so intense yet serene. "Last week I was heading home after class—it was a beautiful fall day—and instead of thinking about the lecture and discussion, or what work I needed to do that night, or even what to have for dinner, I was thinking of Dorsey Furniture and the new accounting system, writing an email to Will in my head on things to set up and how to do it. I was thinking of Granny and her homey kitchen. Above all, I was thinking of you, the fire tower, and *that* kiss." *Sigh.* "That one amazing kiss and dreading my next class. Dreading the projects and reading ahead. All the feels from my summer visit were gone. I had no motivation for school. The two years I was sick, all I *wanted* was to get on with my life and finish my education. Which I did. And in that space, I equated living with education and the acclaim of letters behind my name. Ryder, I *do* want to get on with my life." She glanced down at the pavement and kicked at a small stone. "With you. If you'll have me." There. She'd poured out her heart and—

He snatched her in his arms. "I'm going to kiss you, infection or not."

"I'm not infectious. I had a test before classes started." She pulled a white note from her pocket. "The doctor gave me—"

Ryder's loud and joyful laugh filled her up.

"I love you, Elizabeth Dorsey." His kiss started on her forehead, then down to her cheek and chin, arriving at her lips with such a burning force she couldn't feel the ends of her fingers or toes. He tasted a bit of spearmint and bacon, and his skin radiated a warm hint of soap. Elizabeth held onto his thick shoulders, then slipped one hand to the soft skin on the back of his neck and kissed him back.

Her first real kiss was with the man she'd love forever.

When the kissing finally gave way, he whispered, "Meet me at the fire tower. Six o'clock."

21

Solar lights. Check. Ryder had picked up a set from Sheffield's on his way home.

Blankets and pillows. Check.

The food basket Tina handed him when he went inside to pay for his uneaten lunch. Check.

"A portable charcuterie board," she said. "Cheese, meats, crackers, fruit, and veggies. And a bottle of wine to toast your engagement. Nothing fancy, but it elevates things, don't you think? You *are* going to propose, aren't you? A kiss like *that* says proposal."

Portable speaker he never used? Check.

Playlist of American Standards on his phone. Check.

Ring hidden in the basket. Check.

He'd never admit it to anyone, but he'd googled "romantic proposal" to spark some ideas. Since he left a voicemail proposal from the fire tower, he knew the in-person moment had to be here too. What better place than where they'd shared their unusual and unforgettable first kiss?

Words to say? Not checked. Repeating his voicemail felt uninspired. Coming up with something Shakespearean felt phony. He'd be himself and trust the right moment would come along.

"I love you. Will you marry me?" he whispered over and over until he heard the sound of her footsteps on the tower stairs.

"Hey," she said, stepping into the fire tower cabin.

"Hey." He slapped his hands against his jeans, nervous.

"The tower looks great." She smiled. "I love the lights and pillows. Is that Tina's charcuterie menu?"

"Yeah, she gave it to me when I—"

"Ryder," Elizabeth said, setting down her handbag by the blankets and pillows. "I'm sorry I didn't answer you. It was rude and cowardly. Selfish. I don't want to be that kind of woman."

"To be fair, a voicemail proposal deserved a bit of silence." He pressed play on his phone, and the melody of "As Time Goes By" filled the square box. "Can I have this dance?"

Elizabeth stepped into his arms and rested her head on his shoulder as they turned in a slow sway.

"Granny prayed with me," she said, leaning back to see his face. "To know God's heart."

"And what did God say?"

"I'm here, aren't I?"

Ryder ended the dance. "But not because you need a new goal? Or feel like you have a future, so I'm it?"

"Maybe, a little. I'm still me, Ryder Donovan." She gripped his hand. "But truth is, I'm completely head over heels in love with you. The women in my class complained ad nauseam about not being able to find a good man, yet I'd let one go."

Ryder gathered her to him again and buried his face against her skin. "Will you be happy in Hearts Bend?"

"I've always been happy in Hearts Bend, Ryder. It just took me a few years to admit it."

The song changed to "Someone to Watch Over Me." Ryder knelt by the basket, reaching in for the ring.

"Beth Dorsey, I'm not sure I can top a voicemail proposal, but now that I'm live and in person..." He opened the ring box. "Will you marry me?"

She dropped to her knees in front of him and held his face in her hands. "Try and stop me, Ryder Donovan."

"Oh, I know better than to—"

She pressed her warm lips to his. "I'm going to need a lot of these."

"Good, I have a lot to give."

Ryder slipped the ring on her finger. "This ring has a story."

"It's so beautiful," she said, her smile brighter than the diamond. "I love stories."

After a few more kisses—well, a lot of kisses—they settled into the pile of pillows and dug into the charcuterie basket. While dining on cheese and crackers, prosciutto and salami, grapes and almonds, Elizabeth regaled him with stories of Wharton, and he gave her the latest details on the TWRA investigation.

"The FBI has made a few arrests. A senior accountant at the TWRA had been hiding money for years. Her husband worked at Dorsey Mill. She ordered the cherry and teak using my name, then he fulfilled the orders. Someone else picked it up. She paid the invoices out of a hidden account. They kept the orders below the amount required for authorization by her superiors. She could do it on her own. Then she had to cool her jets and stopped paying for things. Thus, the flagged account at Dorsey." In the distance, a bird sang its song.

"So you're exonerated." Elizabeth rested her head on Ryder's shoulder. "And I'm free from all my striving. Love did that, Ryder. Now tell me about the ring."

He bent forward for a kiss. "Do you know where Earth-n-Treasures used to be?"

The air in the fire tower cabin shifted, and the bird singing the song rested on the tower steps as he told her about the mysterious Jewell and the gift of the ring.

"I tried to return it, but the new owner said he'd never seen it before. Said he couldn't buy it from me 'cause he didn't have the capital yet. We went round and round, me trying to return it and the man saying he couldn't afford to buy it."

"So this ring just showed up at your house? That's crazy." She held her hand up to the evening light. "I don't understand. Who is Jewell, and why'd she give you the ring?"

"I don't know, but I think I have to simply have faith and believe."

"Simple faith?" she said. "That's hard for me."

"Then let's do it together. For the rest of our lives." He kissed her again, sealing their love to the gravelly sounds of Jimmy Durante singing "As Time Goes By."

———— ♥ ————

All her life, she'd believed that if she worked hard enough, she'd achieve her dream. That's what *they* said. And in so many ways, *they* were right. Except *they* forgot to mention life's greatest achievement: love.

It'd been a week since Ryder proposed. Since then, they'd gone to Boston to meet her parents. Ryder pulled Dad aside to ask for his blessing, which he gave. Mom thought Ryder hung the moon, and Jonathan said, "He's okay. I'll accept him as a brother."

Last night, they'd dined at Ryder's with his parents. He grilled kabobs and made his soon-to-be-famous chocolate cake. Or so Elizabeth claimed.

When his mom asked to see the ring, she said, "Oh, good, you found your great-aunt Georgia's ring. I was afraid it'd been sold along with her estate when she died." Mrs. Donovan turned to Elizabeth. "She never had children and was always partial to Ryder. A woman of faith too. Believed God moved in mysterious ways. I'm quite envious of that these days."

Elizabeth exchanged a glance with Ryder. "You mean this ring belonged to your family?"

"Yes, but in all the hubbub of storing and selling, we thought we'd lost it. I was heartsick about it. Ryder, where'd you find it?"

"In the corner of the kitchen counter." He winked at Elizabeth and covered her hand with his.

That moment, she began to truly believe in the love and mystery of God.

Today Elizabeth was executing the rest of her fall-in-love-move-to-Hearts-Bend plan. Dressed in a soft-gray suit with a white blouse and heels, she headed down to Granny's kitchen.

"Look at you," Granny said. "Dressed like a boss."

"I have an interview." She poured a cup of coffee to go.

"In town? Where? Does Will know?"

"Not yet." Elizabeth snatched a slice of toast from the pile Granny had just buttered. "I'll be home for dinner. Ryder is coming over."

"Have you picked a wedding date? You know the Wedding Chapel is booked a year or more out."

"We've talked to Taylor. She'll fit us in. We can get married on a Friday night or Sunday afternoon." Elizabeth kissed Granny, then headed for the mudroom exit. "I actually love living in a town where everyone knows my name. If not mine, someone in the family."

Down River Road, with the radio playing softly, Elizabeth Dorsey whispered a prayer for the day, trying to talk to God a bit more.

At the next light, she turned left into Dorsey Furniture and parked in a visitor slot. Checking her appearance in the rearview mirror, she stepped out of her VW Bug with her messenger bag, résumé inside.

At the front desk, the receptionist, Harmony, greeted her with a quizzical look.

"Elizabeth? What are you doing here?"

"Is Will in?"

"In his office."

Elizabeth knocked on his door.

"Hey, come in. You're back from Boston. Did your dad give his blessing?" But he knew the answer. Pops had announced it in the family chat.

Elizabeth gently set her résumé on his desk. "I'd like

to interview for the CFO job. For when Dan Harper retires."

"I see." Will picked up her résumé. "Okay, Miss Dorsey, have a seat."

For the first time in her life, Elizabeth Dorsey understood how all the paths of her life had led her to this moment: to Ryder, to Hearts Bend, to who she was meant to be.

sleepy Hearts Bend, Tennessee to care for her cancer-stricken mother.

But some people are worth coming home for.

Enter Sam Hardy—the NFL superstar quarterback who crushed her teenage dreams and is now her boss at Haven's Bakery. Once the golden boy who broke her fifteen-year-old heart, he's now fighting his own demons: a playboy reputation he's desperate to shed and a bitter feud with his father that's poisoned his soul. When Chloe walks back into his life—still beautiful, still wounded, still the only woman who ever saw the real him—everything changes.

In Hearts Bend, Tennessee, some hearts get a second chance at forever...

As Chloe throws herself into saving the beloved local bakery from corporate takeover, and Sam fights to prove he's more than his past mistakes, they discover that some loves are worth waiting fifteen years for. But when Chloe's late husband leaves her a stunning surprise that could pull her back to France forever, she must choose between honoring her past and embracing an uncertain future.

Sometimes the biggest risk isn't protecting your heart—it's having the courage to open it again.

"A masterful blend of heartbreak and hope that will leave you believing in the transformative power of love. Chloe and Sam's story is pure magic." —Rachel Hauck, New York Times bestselling author

Perfect for fans of:
Nicholas Sparks • Debbie Macomber • Susan Mallery

💔 **Second chance romance that heals**
🤍 **Small-town meets superstar**
🧁 **A bakery worth fighting for**
🕊️ **Love that transcends loss**

231

When love calls twice, will you answer?

Get your copy today and fall in love with Hearts Bend!

Anyone But You was previously published in 2022 as *One Fine Day*.

ANYONE BUT YOU

SNEAK PEEK

Chapter 1

Of all the things Chloe LaRue had ever dreamed she'd be doing on a fine Monday afternoon in February, folding laundry in her old bedroom wasn't one of them.

Married to a handsome athlete of some kind? Maybe. Living in Paris? Oh, she'd hoped so. Making a name for herself as a pastry chef, maybe even owning her own café? Definitely.

She'd achieved most of these things, her dreams, until life kicked her to the curb.

Baking petit fours during the day and dancing in clubs with her gorgeous, extreme sports competitor husband all night, sure.

But thirty and widowed and moving back home to take care of her mother? Never saw that one coming.

She dropped the laundry basket on her bed and looked around. Mom hadn't changed much in here, other than replacing the ratty old carpet. The walls were still a loud purple, the bookcase stuffed with her old journals, and the Jimmy Eat World poster with curling and brown edges remained taped to the closet door.

Whoever said starting over, having a clean slate, was a good thing? Probably the same wise guy who said time heals all wounds. Because neither seemed to be happening for her.

She slid open the closet door and laughed softly. There were her Doc Martens, still on the floor in the exact spot she'd left them after graduating from Rock Mill High. Her studded belts still hung from the closet hooks, and her black emo clothes remained on the hangers.

If only she could go back and tell that lonely, angst-filled teenager to lighten up, to give herself—and others—a little grace. That girl who'd wanted to be different yet the same as everyone else had found herself in culinary school, and it was the best of both worlds. Her emo roots—the only Fall Out Boy fan in a school of Carrie Underwood wannabes—had given her the strength and fortitude for life in a fast-paced, high-pressure kitchen. For life as a pastry chef.

Chloe pulled a black hoodie off the hanger to make room for her red wool coat.

Oh Mom, you've changed so few things since I left. But why would she? Mom had lost so much. Chloe didn't blame her for hanging onto precious things. Like preserving her daughter's room. Chloe never dreamed she'd lose a second man she loved. That she'd end up widowed, just like Mom.

A week ago, she'd been spinning hot caramel into birds' nests to adorn cakes as the pastry chef at Bistro

Gaspard, a small but highly regarded restaurant in the Bastille district of Paris. Then Mom called. *"So...I have a little bit of cancer."* Chloe had dropped everything and returned to sleepy, slow, country-touristy Hearts Bend, Tennessee.

She'd lost her father when she was eight. Then her husband ten months ago, when she was twenty-nine. She flat refused to lose her mother. She'd will her to live, or—cue the irony and cliché—die trying.

A meow rustled the silence of the room and Chloe turned to see Honey, Mom's ginger cat, curled up on the bed. She stared at Chloe as if she understood her thoughts and spoke up to keep her from tumbling down into the familiar dark hole of pity and sadness.

"I'm working on it, Honey. I promise."

Honey narrowed her hazel-green eyes, waited a second, then seemingly satisfied, stretched and tucked her head into the crook of a leg.

A bit of light broke through the February clouds and leaked into the room, dripping over the window seat where Chloe used to read and dream about a life beyond her tiny hometown. Marriage. A pastry career. Maybe even her own café or bistro someday. She smiled, breathing easy, feeling free, at least for now, of the burdens she'd brought with her from France. The bare branches of the tree outside her second-story bedroom window allowed dim sunshine to puddle on the newly installed beige carpet.

But she didn't have time for pondering or the heart for any more painful memories, so she tipped over the laundry basket and settled down to folding as the sun retreated behind the clouds again. She snapped a cotton

T-shirt and smoothed out the wrinkles. Coming home to help Mom didn't mean she was *moving* backward, right? Coming home allowed her to regroup, pass Go, collect her two hundred dollars, and—in a few months—get back in the pastry chef game.

Coming home meant she was looking *forward.*

Her earlier life, with its hopes and dreams, had ended so suddenly. She and Jean-Marc had talked of purchasing a café, had that odd, pointless argument about money, then she had found herself suddenly swallowed up by the dark pain of a graveside goodbye. The confusion of their emptied bank account and papers shoved at her to sign only solidified her feelings of loss and despair. The papers that her in-laws assured her were formalities needed to settle Jean-Marc's shares of the family business. When the whirlwind had settled, she'd faced the abrupt starkness of empty days without the man she loved.

Oh Jean-Marc, I'm sorry...so, so sorry.

Within weeks, the joy of blending flour, sugar, and butter into macarons, croissants, and èclairs had become a weight. Simple things like piping icing on a petit four became a laborious task. She battled a thick mental fog, and nothing seemed to nurse her broken heart. Getting out of bed felt like a chore. Chloe paced all night and slept all day, calling in sick to work often. Even when the sun was shining, her grief made it seem as though the whole world was cloudy. She thought she was going crazy. Often, she felt as though she was dying as well.

A colleague had recommended a grief support group, which she reluctantly joined. The leader assured her all she felt was normal. But if this was *normal*, she wanted out. What was the point of living when all her dreams—a café of their own and a cottage in the French countryside—were buried six feet in the ground with her husband?

Her breaking point had come last month, when she found herself lying on the couch of her cold apartment, calling Jean-Marc's phone just to hear his voicemail greeting. She would end up weeping and inhaling a faint trace of his scent in the threads of the old quilt. Then she'd remembered the good times, how he'd finally believed in her dream to own a café in Deux Jardins— and the grief started all over again.

When Mom called, it was as if life, fate, or perhaps God had taken pity on her and delivered her from the tomb of *Life and Love Lost*. Breast cancer, Mom said, trying to sound chipper. Chloe couldn't pack fast enough. She'd loaded suitcases and boxes with her rolling pins and cake pans, dishes, photos, one ridiculously expensive men's watch, clothes, and mementos of the life she'd built with Jean-Marc. She found herself buying a one-way ticket home.

Okay, Chloe, enough. No more dwelling on the past. Look to the future. However bleak and barren it may be.

For the next few minutes, she set up house in her old room, layering her old dresser drawers with her clean shirts, jeans and shorts, socks and undies, hanging up her coats and dresses—the remnants of her Paris life an odd juxtaposition to the girl she'd once been.

"Honey..." She held the laundry basket in her hand and smiled at the cat. "I'm leaving now. Keep my bed warm, okay?" Hand on the light switch, she was about to turn off the lamp when a glint of sunshine burst through the trees, bounced off the dresser mirror, and illuminated the row of pictures tucked into the mirror's edge. Chloe set the basket in the hallway, then crossed the room and leaned in for a closer look at the official photo of her high school cast and crew of *The Importance of Being Earnest*. Oh boy, that had been a fun production. She'd been in her "I'm a unique emo girl" element as a stagehand for the high school play, working behind the scenes, pulling the curtains, adjusting props.

JoJo Castle—Mathews, now—had played Gwendolen Fairfax. JoJo always won the female leads, but she had the talent and was always sweet to the crew, never stuck-up or snobby. Would she still be the same since she'd married Buck Mathews, the biggest artist in country music? Chloe imagined she'd find out since Buck and JoJo lived in Hearts Bend when he wasn't on tour. They were bound to run into each other in the town square.

Chloe replaced the picture in the mirror's brown, wooden frame and pulled out the next one—a photo-booth strip taken at the fair that summer before their senior year. She and Sam Hardy made faces at the camera and each other. Sam...with his dark hair and deep brown eyes. Did he still have the stubborn curl that fell on his forehead? He'd done well, *really* well, as a first-round draft pick from University of Tennessee to the Titans. He'd been their franchise quarterback ever since.

Oooh, I had such a crush on you back in the day, Sammy.

She reached for the framed photo of Daddy on the dresser. How she'd love to feel his arms around her in one of his bear hugs, to bake his favorite pound cake for him one more time, to talk to him about Jean-Marc. She may have only known him for eight years, but Daddy had always made things better. He was her hero.

I miss you so much, Daddy. She ran a finger over the image of his hair, which was a tad too long for a hustling businessman, but he loved his ole '70s style. She smiled and tsked.

Now you're forever shaggy, Daddy.

A soft knock sounded at the door and Mom poked her head in. "Can I help with anything?" Her gaze drifted to Daddy's photo. "You remember when that was taken? At his last company picnic." She didn't speak the obvious. *A few weeks before he was killed.* "Twenty-two years and I still miss him."

Mom came the rest of the way into the room and picked up a different photo. One of Chloe and Jean-Marc at their wedding, coming down the aisle after the minister pronounced them husband and wife, their arms raised in victory. "I didn't know I'd left this here," Mom said softly. "I'll take it—"

"Mom, it's okay." Chloe set the gilded frame back on the dresser. She liked her expression in the photo. Would she ever smile that proudly, that excitedly again? "It's been almost a year since he died. I can see our picture without falling apart." But only recently. "Besides, I look really good here."

Mom laughed and after a second, Chloe joined her. Also only recently, she'd started to laugh again. Which seemed a sort of consolation prize for leaving Paris: her job, her memories, even her in-laws, whom she loved.

Being in Hearts Bend gave her a little window on life. Some semblance of home. Maybe she'd find the freedom to dream again.

"I have more photos with my things." Chloe glanced around the room toward her boxes, spied the one she wanted, and pulled out her favorite wedding photo, an image of her and Jean-Marc with their parents. "You looked beautiful, *Maman*, in your vintage Dior dress. Vivienne and Albert"—she gave the soft French pronunciation, Al-bare—"were so gracious and welcoming to us."

The five of them stood outside the old stone church near the LaRue family villa in Provence. Lavender fields behind them shimmered in the sun. In this photograph, Chloe smiled up at Jean-Marc while he gazed down at her with a tender expression. She remembered how his eyes had shone with love. They had been happy, so happy that day.

So how did it all end in a sudden death after a massive argument? There were moments when she couldn't really remember who had started the debate, or why. It had just seemed to snowball like an avalanche...

Chloe winced, a cold heartache pricking her moment of peace, and set the picture back in the box.

"Can we set this one out?" Mom retrieved it. "I think it will help you to grieve and recover if you remember the good times, darling."

"Y-yeah, sure." Mom knew some of the story of how Jean-Marc had died. But not all of it. Chloe peered in the box and, seeing Jean-Marc's watch, reached for it. This wretched thing had caused their first big fight, a few months after the wedding. She'd been furious when he told her what he'd paid for it.

"Why? You don't need it. A watch meant for scuba diving

with what, a chronograph and chronometer? You're a rock climber, Jean-Marc, a skier, not a scuba diver."

"Not yet, no. But I will be, chère cœur. Soon."

What a silly thing to fight about. If he wanted the watch so he could learn to scuba dive safely, he should have it. It was for his *safety*, after all. She set the watch on her dresser next to the photo. *Their* photo. Husband and wife. The couple who had stood in the chapel and pledged their love for as long as they lived.

An image flashed across her mind from Jean-Marc's graveside service—which happened every time she wandered any distance down memory lane. A blonde woman speaking with her in-laws in hushed tones and how they'd quieted and glanced at one another dubiously when Chloe approached. But she'd caught the whispered *"affaire de cœur"* hanging in the air.

Affair of the heart.

"Chloe? Are you all right?" Mom roped her arm around Chloe's shoulder. "Are you glad to be home? Truly?"

"Yeah, um, I'm fine." Mom had been there that day as well, but she'd seen and heard nothing. If she had, she would've asked. That was Mom's way. "I'm truly glad to be home. I couldn't let you go through cancer treatment on your own. I'm where I need to be."

Mom's eyes glistened as she looked away. For her, Chloe knew, talking about the next months and year only made her diagnosis all too real. Too threatening.

"Did you see the rest of the pictures on the mirror?" Mom said, leaning in, hands clasped behind her back. "I've only dusted around them for the past decade." Mom motioned to the strip of Chloe and Sam. "I remember that summer. You and Sam spent hours in the Hardys' pool while I was learning his father's business, training to be his admin." Mom had been working for Frank Hardy, Sam's dad, ever since.

"Does Sam still call his dad Frank?" Until Chloe had seen the old stage crew picture and the photo strip, she'd not thought of her teenage friends in ages. Except Sam. Jean-Marc was a fan of American football and enjoyed telling his football-loving friends *his* wife had attended high school with the great Sam Hardy. Jean-Marc kept up with Sam via sports websites as well as the good ole *Hearts Bend Tribune*, which bragged about their home-town boy every chance they got. Jean-Marc recited details about Sam's successes, and they'd talked of a trip home last summer to see Mom, explore Chloe's childhood haunts, and of course, arrange an introduction to Sam.

"As far as I know he still does," Mom said. "Sam rarely comes home. Frank mentions him once in a while, but I'm sure he misses him, even if he's too proud to admit it."

"Sounds like they're both stubborn."

"In a word, yes." Mom laughed as she turned to peek into one of Chloe's boxes lined up along the wall. "Try working for one of them. Ooo, your teddy bear." Mom reached in for the trusty old stuffed animal, the one Chloe had moved halfway around the world—*twice*.

"For your bed," Mom said, her eyes glistening again.

She'd had the bear made from Dad's favorite flannel shirt, and Chloe liked to imagine his fragrance still resided in the threads. Maybe she'd have another made from Jean-Marc's dark blue thermal. Keep them both on her bed, make it a memorial. She shook her head, throwing off depressing thoughts.

"It's about dinner time," Mom said. "Are you hungry? We could run to Ella's Diner. Tina

reinstated Monday night pie nights. If we go early, we can get a booth by the front window."

Chloe sighed and sat on the edge of the bed, a fresh batch of tears rising.

Mom placed a hand on Chloe's arm. "What is it, darling?"

She flopped backward onto the old soft quilt. "Just this…life. I don't mind being here, I want to be here, honest. But I can't get it out of my head entirely that this is not what I planned on doing when I was turning thirty. I've been a mess since Jean-Marc died. One minute I'm angry at him. The next, weeping and sobbing and missing him so much, it physically pains my chest. I feel like I'm having a heart attack."

Mom lay down next to her and Chloe rested her head on Mom's shoulder. "You know what I'm going to say, don't you?"

Chloe sat up. "Yes, so don't." She wasn't ready to hear—*again*—that she'd get over losing her husband, she'd go on with life, maybe even find a new love. Yada, yada. *Whatever.* Clearly Mom didn't practice what she preached. Twenty-two years after Daddy died, she was still alone.

Alone. Which was another reason why Chloe had left Paris to come home and help Maman.

"Why don't we bake tomorrow? That always cheered you up as a girl."

Chloe's eyes filled with tears. "MeMaw's vanilla cake?"

Mom kissed her forehead. "That's the one. Unless you've come up with some fancy French pastry that cures your blues."

"No way. MeMaw's cake is the *only* thing to soothe a sad soul."

"So, dinner?" Mom elbowed Chloe's side. "Ella's?"

Chloe surveyed the boxes stacked under the window seat—the ones she'd shipped at an exorbitant fee from France—and considered more unpacking. But where would she put the dishes or linens she'd acquired in her life as an ex-pat? The remnants of nearly eight years with Jean-Marc. She was here for now but not staying forever. This was just to get herself together and to see Mom through chemo and radiation.

Chloe drew a breath with a side glance at Mom. Now was as good a time as ever. "We've talked about Dad's death, Jean-Marc, my return home, dinner, and vanilla cake, but not why I'm really here."

Mom got up and moved to the window. "You know why. I feel like if I talk about it, I'm feeding it. If I ignore it, maybe it will go away." She looked at Chloe. "Silly, I know."

"Not silly. I understand." Chloe slipped off the bed. "What time is your appointment in the morning?" The what-to-expect-during-treatment appointment would be Chloe's first opportunity to introduce herself to Mom's medical team. Chemo would start officially the next day.

"Nine o'clock. I hope you don't regret coming home from Paris to chauffeur me to the doctor or chemo clinic.

I'm glad you're home, don't get me wrong, I just wish it wasn't to take care of me. What about your career?"

"You are more important than my career. At least death has taught me one good lesson. Besides, I wasn't in the right mind to make any more of my position at the bistro. This change to start over might spark something new, something different and good. Mostly I came home because you have cancer and need support. Mom, you were always there for me, now let me be there for you."

"I'm the mother. Of course, I was there for you. But you're supposed to be out living your life, having babies, buying a home, and becoming a world-famous pastry chef."

Chloe scoffed. "Well, life saw fit to do otherwise and there is no place I'd rather be. Fame, ah, it'll wait for me." She glanced toward the photo booth strip she'd taken with Sam Hardy. "I bet if you ask him, fame is way overrated anyway."

Mom turned away, brushing the back of her hand over her cheeks. "All this mush is making me hungry. I'll get my pocketbook and we can go."

"Sounds good." Chloe reached for her handmade leather bucket bag she and Jean-Marc had found at a custom shop in the French countryside, and her favorite beret. She looked again at the boxes. Tomorrow. She would unpack tomorrow. If she'd learned anything from death, it was to not worry over the small things.

"Does Ella's still have fabulous milk shakes?" Chloe followed Mom down the stairs.

"You bet." At the coat rack, Mom and Chloe pulled on their winter coats before stepping into the Tennessee cold. "Let's walk. Ella's isn't far."

— ♥ —

Their brisk walk was under a blue winter sky laced with the gold, red, and orange of the setting sun. Each step brought memories of running and playing down this lane with her friends. Riding her bike in the summer and throwing snowballs at the neighbor boy, Landon Martin, in the winter. She'd read in the latest Rock Mill High alumni newsletter he was a Wall Street mover and shaker now.

"Hearts Bend was a great place to grow up, Mom." Chloe slipped her arm through her mother's. "I have so many good memories."

"I'm glad. Hearts Bend is a great little town."

They turned off Red Oak Lane and headed down First Avenue. Across the way, Gardenia Park slept under a blanket of old snow. Mom's breath billowed about her head as she chattered and pointed out the new ice-cream flavors Pop's Yer Uncle Ice Cream Shop advertised in the window—Peppermint and Vanilla Sweetheart—as well as the pretty twinkle lights glowing inside Valentino's restaurant, the donut and muffin-shaped paper cutouts on the plate glass window, along with a placard propped on the sill of Haven's Bakery. Oh, she had a million memories of Saturday mornings at Haven's with Mom.

The more they walked, the more Chloe's memories surfaced, and she was awash with sentimentality. By the time they entered Ella's, she almost believed coming home was just the tonic she needed to shoo away the rags of death. Here she could ground herself in the truths that raised her.

Tina, Ella's pretty and peppy owner, approached with two menus and surprise in her eyes. "Chloe! My goodness, the famous French pastry chef graces my humble diner." Tina's hug felt like a warm drink on a cold, blustery day.

"Stop, I'm not famous. Not even close." Chloe slid into the second booth from the door and glanced out over Gardenia Circle, the park, and the slotted parking spaces filling up with folks coming to dine after a long workday. "But I do owe you for letting me bake and sell MeMaw's vanilla cake here. Remember that?"

"I sure do. Even back then you were a whiz in the kitchen. And darling, 'round here, anyone who makes it as the pastry chef in a Michelin-starred Paris restaurant is a big whomping deal." Tina handed Chloe and then Mom a menu. "Meredith, how you feeling? I've been praying for you."

"I'm fine, but I'll take all the prayers I can get."

"I'll be back with some waters, then y'all can order." Tina propped her hand on her hip. "Welcome home, Chloe."

The simple sentiment hit Chloe in the chest and her eyes flooded. Mom stretched her hands across the table and squeezed Chloe's arm but, like the wise woman she was, said nothing. Chloe reached for a tissue in her bag as Mom saw a couple across the way and went over to say hi, which led to her talking to the couple in another booth and the big, long table of what looked like town council members.

Look at you, Mom. She looked more like a council

candidate than a woman battling a cancer diagnosis. But Chloe had seen the mammogram, read the biopsy report, talked to the oncologist while she was still in Paris.

"Fast growing, but caught early"—thank You, God—*"very treatable."*

So. Mom had cancer. People survived cancer all the time. Still, the thought stabbed icy fear into Chloe's heart. She took a deep breath and smiled as Mom's laugh echoed around the diner. She would be okay. She had to be.

Chloe dug in her bag for another tissue. Instead of the soft-pack that had taken up a recent permanent residence in there, her fingers brushed a stiff piece of paper, down at the bottom, wedged into the corner seam. With a gentle tug, it came free, and she smoothed it open on the table.

Oh my. She'd forgotten she'd stuck that list in her purse. How many months ago? Well over a year, it had to be. Our Goals for the Year, written in her neat script.

Jean-Marc's list focused on business: *Convince Papa to hire a social media manager. Research and contract with new microfiber vendor.* Hers covered both her job and her marriage: *Institute mentoring/coaching at restaurant. Weekly dates. Save 20% of our income for the café.*

A tear landed on the page, smudging the percentage sign. She remembered now. She had put the list in her purse to have it laminated, so it wouldn't curl and fade when she taped it to their bathroom mirror. But she'd forgotten about it. And then every time she had made a savings deposit, the balance was less than the last time. By the time she'd figured out Jean-Marc was making withdrawals, she'd been about to open a separate account to save for the café.

She crumpled up the list and stuffed it back into her bag as the waitress, Spicy, brought two glasses of water to the table. Chloe ordered a burger, fries, and a chocolate shake. Mom hurried over to say she'd have the same.

When Spicy left, Mom squared off with Chloe, that *mother* look in her eye. "You always tried to take care of me. It was cute when you were ten and endearing when you were sixteen. But now you're thirty and I do need some support. I admit it. We will get through this together, but darling daughter, I can't have you hovering and worrying. You'll drive me bonkers. So, here's an idea." Mom drew a deep breath and gave Chloe a tremulous smile. "Why don't you get a job?"

Titans need a new franchise QB. One with two working knees. @SamHardyQB15's career seems to be fading along with his knees. Save the $$ and give it to someone who can bring home the ring. #dump-SamHardy – @No.1TitanFan on Twitter

ACKNOWLEDGMENTS

Thanks to Susan May Warren, my writing partner for twenty-two years, for challenging me to write a simple, sweet romance. Much appreciation to all the Sunrise staff and their amazing work.

ABOUT RACHEL HAUCK

New York Times, USA Today & Wall Street Journal Bestselling author Rachel Hauck writes from sunny central Florida. A RITA finalist and winner of Romantic Times Inspirational Novel of the Year, and Career Achievement Award, she writes vivid characters dealing with real life issues. Readers have fallen in love with the quaint and loveable small town of Hearts Bend, TN introduced in the Romantic Times Top Pick and Christy Award-winning novel, *The Wedding Chapel*. Visit her at www.rachelhauck.com.

facebook.com/rachelhauck

instagram.com/rachelhauck

x.com/rachelhauck

bookbub.com/authors/rachel-hauck

amazon.com/stores/author/B001IXRSKS

CONNECT WITH SUNRISE

Thank you so much for reading *When I'm With You*. We hope you enjoyed the story. If you did, would you be willing to do us a favor and leave a review? It doesn't have to be long—just a few words to help other readers know what they're getting. (But no spoilers! We don't want to wreck the fun!) Thank you again for reading!

We'd love to hear from you—not only about this story, but about any characters or stories you'd like to read in the future. Contact us at www.sunrisepublishing. com/contact.

We also have a regular updates that contains sneak peeks, reviews, upcoming releases, and fun stuff for our reader friends. Sign up at www.sunrisepublishing.com or scan our QR code.

scan me
sunrisepublishing.com

Welcome to
Redemption, Alaska

Where broken hearts come to heal

PUBLISHERS WEEKLY BESTSELLING AUTHOR

Heidi McCahan

We solve the problem of what to read next.

Home to Heritage

SUSAN MAY WARREN and **TARI FARIS**

with **Mandy Boerma** and **Andrea Michelle Wood**

We solve the problem of what to read next.

YOU MAY ALSO LIKE...

When Noah Hebert inherits the struggling Blue Pirogue Inn, he must solve a puzzle left by his grandfather to save it from his family's nemesis, Isaac Bergeron. Teaming up with Elisa Bergeron, the café manager and his rival, they must navigate family feuds—and unexpected sparks—while racing against time.

Where I Found You by Besty St. Amant

Working together to keep Fox Bakery from going under, Robin and Sammy find that something more than friendship is simmering between them. But will Robin follow her old dreams back to the glamor of Paris, or will she discover how sweet it is to be loved in Deep Haven?

How Sweet It Is by Andrea Christenson

Dani Sullivan is determined to revive Jonathon Island's fading charm and reunite her fractured family. Her plan? Reopen the Grand Sullivan Hotel. But without the funds to restore the hotel, Dani's forced to accept help from Liam Stone—a big-city hotel developer whose sleek, modern vision is everything she's trying to avoid.

Meet Me at the Grand by Lindsay Harrel

We solve the problem of what to read next.

WHERE EVERY STORY IS A FRIEND, AND EVERY CHAPTER IS A NEW JOURNEY...

Subscribe to our newsletter for a free book, the latest news, weekly giveaways, exclusive author interviews, and more!

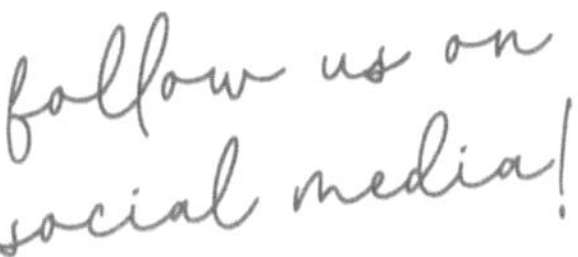

Shop paperbacks, ebooks, audiobooks, and more at
SUNRISEPUBLISHING.MYSHOPIFY.COM